ETCHED

Britt Nunes

Published by

Martin Sisters Publishing, LLC

www. martinsisterspublishing. com

Copyright © 2013 Britt Nunes

To my twin sister - who keeps reading.

ACKNOWLEDGEMENTS

I want to give one BIG THANK YOU!!! To all my family and friends!!!

To my Mom - who sat and listened to me read *Etched*. Your anticipating and anxious facial expressions will forever be embedded in my mind.

To Steve Sonntag - who helped TREMENDOUSLY with editing. I will always be grateful for the mini-tutor sessions.

To my twin sister - there are no words (go figure). You are my best brainstorming helper and bulldozer for writer's block.

Prologue

"Shh, you're safe now."

I flapped my arms like a bird helplessly trying to fly away, but my wings were broken. I was trapped inside this liquid prison, fighting against a cold and vicious swamp, not knowing how I got there. Empty. Numb. Nothing made sense. The only thing I could hold on to were the words that echoed in my mind. Shh, you're safe now. My brain was broken; it melted into sludge and oozed out of my ears, making everything that was in it sink to the bottom of the swamp—out of reach. I couldn't remember anything before this moment. It was all a void covered in gooey mud.

In the blackness, I felt a firmer chunk of soil. I began clawing my fingers into the soft, wet earth. It was a slow and painful process, but I was able to pull most of my body onto an alien shoreline. As I lay huffing and gasping for air, my skin prickled and knitted together. My right hand felt strangely empty, like it was waiting for someone to touch it. Green, silver, trees, and plastic masks—everything was just…fading away. A sob crawled up my throat but couldn't reach my lips.

My limbs started trembling mercilessly as the cold midnight encircled me, turning everything to ice. The mud that was caked all over my skin began to freeze, and the air leeched what little warmth I had left inside my body.

"Oh, Mylanta!" a deep, booming voice shouted above my chattering teeth.

"Is everything all right, Erin?" A high, female voice shouted next.

"It's a girl, Maggs. There's a little girl over here!"

"Erin, stay right there," said the woman. "Erin. Erin. Don't touch her. She might be contaminated by the sewage," the woman said, making strides in my direction.

"Maggie." His voice had a sour note to it.

The man stepped closer to me, and with the sound of swishing cloth, rough wool encompassed me. My shivers became filled with fear; my lump of a sob was still caught somewhere between my teeth and tongue. A pair of sturdy arms wrapped around me, and the smell of musky earth filled my nose. My whole body started to ache and burn with heat. I wanted warmth, but not some musky flames that consumed me as if I were kindling. My mind melted further into slush, a confusing and murky slop of mush. Silver. Plastic masks. Shh, you're safe now. I was trying to hold on to what little remained in my brain, but everything felt as solid as air.

"Oh, my goodness," the woman gasped. Her voice was full of pity.

"It's gonna be okay, kid." The man smiled down at me.

As he got to his feet with me cradled in his arms, the woman came into view.

"I think she has hypothermia." The woman's rough features melted with her sentence, and she began to reach for me with a kind hand. But she dropped her hand and squared her shoulders. Her voice rolled out, strict and emotionless. "We need to get her back to the Manor."

*

I must have blacked out, because the next thing I knew, I was lying in the backseat of a car as the woman vigorously dried my hair with some kind of coarse fabric. She dabbed mud from my face and neck. I cracked my eyes open and saw her hair tucked securely behind her ear. Her eyes were intense and focused. Her jaw was tightly set, making her cheeks look brutally angular.

She wiped off my right arm and started working on my left. When she began cleaning the dirt from my forearm, her hands suddenly froze, and a small gasp tumbled from her lips.

"Erin," her voice came out in a quiver.

"We're here," he said, putting the car in park.

"Erin?"

"Good, ole Betsy still gots some juice left in her," he said with a small, forced smile in his voice as he patted the top of the dashboard.

"Erin?"

"What, Maggs?" He turned around, and I saw his face drop. "What's wrong?"

"Look," she said holding out my arm.

His reaction was something between a horrified gasp and a petrified huff. He closed his eyes as if he wanted to erase what he had just seen.

"She's been etched," the woman whispered.

I stared at the woman's hands as she held my arm out to the man. My eyes shifted to my forearm, and on my skin, irrevocably written, were deep lines of scar tissue.

The woman took a hard gulp of air. "What do we do?"

As the man opened his eyes, his face became severe, and his voice rumbled low in his throat. "Cover it up."

One

White cloth.
Untarnished metallic.
Plastic masks.
Blurry figures.
"Shh, you're safe now."

A warm hand gripped my fingers tightly and pulled me through a canopy of trees. I heard a mechanical growl echo in the darkness. Suddenly, everything shifted and I was standing in a room, staring at the branches of a tree that grew along the ceiling. Its massive roots made a jagged fracture in the floorboards. My world shifted again. The warm hand held my fingers firmly as it pulled me through slippery terrain. Mud flew up with each panicked stride and spattered across my body. I slipped, and my fingertips lost their grip. I was flying, a freedom I felt as my feet escaped the ground. Then gravity snagged me and began yanking me down, and I was falling. Everything moved in slow motion, and all I could see in the blackness were the scarred lines on my forearm. I broke past the surface of a swamp. Cold, thick liquid encompassed me, forcing me to take an abrupt breath.

*

I awoke choking and gasping for air, still able to feel the frigid licks of the swamp across my skin, inside my lungs. For a split second—the state in between sleep and wakefulness—I thought I was still in the swamp, still waiting for Madam and Erin to find me. A heartbeat later, I was in my room, twisted in my familiar comforter in my bed, just as I'd done for the last eight years. I rolled over. My pillowcase was damp from perspiration —chilled, liquid fear. My gaze turned to my dark green sweatband, the one I wore snugly around my left forearm. Curiosity pulled at my insides as I stared at the fraying, absorbent fabric. I'd worn it for so long, it felt as comfortable as my own skin. I took a quick survey of my surroundings. Just blankets, pillows, and me. After sucking in a mouthful of air, I pulled down my sweatband to expose my etching.

It seemed small to me, only two inches wide as it wrapped around my forearm like a manacle, tiny enough to be hidden behind a simple sweatband. The delicate skin of my inner forearm was deformed by lines of deep scar tissue in the shape of an asterisk. The tips of the asterisk stretched out so far that it met and melted into its twin on the top of my arm, bowing to link them forever in continuous circles. I skimmed my fingertips over my sleek, raised skin, feeling rebellious and nervous. I'd been conditioned to keep it covered always.

When I heard the sound of footsteps creeping outside my door, I quickly pulled up my sweatband. I heard the soft, hushed taps of sneakers against the old, rasping hardwood floor. There was a light knock on my bedroom door followed by a gentle push.

The door creaked open. "Basil?" whispered Erin.

I turned over in my bed to see Erin standing in the middle of my doorframe. The hallway light outlined his silhouette, making his white hair beam brightly. He wore a thick wool jacket and a pair of jeans with a rip on one of the knees. As soon as I noticed the unit of cables on his shoulder and the tarp tucked under his arm, I quickly shot my head up.

"First rain?" I said with a soft, eager smile, forgetting all about my nightmare.

"Yup. Let's go, kid," Erin said, his voice holding its usual huskiness.

I stumbled out of my bed and practically ran out the door, following Erin through the hallway and down the stairs that led into the kitchen pantry. We headed for the small mudroom leading to the backdoor of the manor. As soon as we pushed past the doorframe, we both took off running. The cool forest air filled my nose with a musky, inviting scent. My next deep breath revealed the smell of rain. The gravel chilled my bare feet as we ran through the backyard toward the cobblestone path that led into the woods.

We hustled down the path and ran through the dark forest, running into the small clearing Erin had made. Six wooden poles protruded from the ground, each four stories high. Erin threw down the unit of cables, and we both started to twine them into the metal rings around the tarp. Securing a cord in my mouth, I scaled up one of the poles onto a small metal platform. The clouds rumbled above me, and as I pulled the cord through the first metal loop, the sky began to weep happy tears onto me. The chill of rain made my appendages move quicker, and my senses seemed hyperaware of my surroundings. I turned on the electric grid that was mounted on the wooden pole. The electric grid, which allowed fresh rainwater to come in but kept germs and other particles out, hummed softly as it came to life. I climbed down and curled the end of the cord around the thick metal nails, anchoring it down with several tights knots. The sky poured down on us relentlessly, turning the dirt to mud as Erin and I worked on the other poles. Soon, the rain catcher started to take form. The large tarp stretched open, dipping low in the center, embracing the droplets from above with comforting hugs.

When we had finished, Erin and I stared at the completed rain catcher wordlessly. Even though we were drenched with rain and mud, neither of us was done with the first shower of the season yet. I glanced down at my feet, which I usually kept bare, and saw mud caked between my toes. A small smile crept across my face, and I took another whiff of rain-filled air.

"Catcher season has officially started," Erin shouted up to the fitful sky, and then pulled me into his arms as if he were the rain catcher and I was the rain. He enfolded my petite frame inside his thick wool jacket. The familiar scent of earth filled my nose, and the fragrance lingered like a stubborn stain. Erin placed his hand atop my head and gave my light brown locks a shake.

"I love the first rain of catcher season," I said crossing my arms over my chest timidly.

"That's cuz you take after me," Erin said as he poked my nose with his index finger. The moon made his pale blue eyes jubilant, and his wrinkles seemed less pronounced.

"Only your good traits," I said with a small, wily smile, but then shyness consumed my body again, making my smile vanish. Looking down I mumbled, "Sorry."

The rain died to a light sprinkle. Erin gazed up into the clouds. We both took deep breaths of crisp air, trying to smell rain, but the sky was done for the time being.

"You should hit the hay. It's late, and we have a lot of rain catchers to set up if we are going to make our water orders this season," Erin said.

"Okay." I took a hesitant breath. "Erin? Thank you for—" I bit my lip, cutting myself off.

Erin chuckled as he tugged me into a bear hug. "It wouldn't seem right doing this without you, Baze. Thank you for helping me out." Erin knew me so well. Sometimes, we'd have full conversations without even saying a word.

"Make sure you wash up before you hit the sheets; otherwise, Maggie will have a cow and three chickens." Erin nudged me in the direction of the manor.

"Okay. I wouldn't want to make Madam mad." Only Erin could get away with calling her Maggie, probably because he was her husband.

"Basil!" Erin shouted after me.

I stopped and turned around.

"Love you, kid."

I smiled and headed off to the manor.

Two

I awoke with my crimson comforter twisted around my torso, my cream-colored sheets mingling with my toes, and my hair splayed across my face, the aftermath of my usual floundering sleep. The smell of rain and cinder tangled with my tendrils. The scent of catcher season taunted me. Swimming through the waves of my comforter, I threw my legs over the edge of my bed and sat up in a drowsy stupor, rubbing sleep from my face and felt a pillow greet my feet.

The dark morning hung in my room, layering everything with a coat of gray. I didn't have much in the way of personal effects—just a bed, a trunk, an armoire, and a mini rain catcher Erin had made for me resting on my windowsill. All the wood was dark oak with plenty of personality, worn-down around the corners and scratched from age. Grabbing my throw blanket, which was hiding under my bed, I headed out of my room.

As I moseyed downstairs, the enticing aroma of Bobby's coffee greeted me. The rich perfume swirled around me, silently declaring that it was a new day. I entered the kitchen and took a seat on one of the stools. The bar table connected to the sink and counter, a front row seat to the entire kitchen. I watched Bobby's back as he frosted a tray of cupcakes that made my mouth water. His shoulders were tensed, his blonde hair unkempt, and his black t-shirt was splattered with flour and a rainbow of buttercream. Bobby was always in the kitchen working on his orders, on delicious food we never could afford to eat.

"Hey, Basil. Shh, give me one more minute to concentrate," Bobby whispered, placing a mug of coffee next to my cupped hands.

I clutched the mug, pressed the rim to my lips, and took a long, slow sip. My face squished up as the taste of dirt slid across my tastebuds. I coughed a couple of times and set the mug down. My morning stupor was suddenly jolted out of me. I glanced inside the mug, remembering that we'd been out of actual coffee grounds for days, and what stared up at me was Bobby's coffee concoction. The concoction was a deceptively beautiful-smelling blend he brewed between outpost trips.

"I have a surprise for you, Baze," Bobby said, slinking over to the counter in front of me, "but it's top secret." He emphasized the secrecy by lowering his voice to a whisper and glanced around the room cautiously.

"My lips are sealed," I said running my index finger and thumb across my lips as if I were zipping them up.

Bobby gave me a wink and slid a small, misshapen cupcake next to my cup of coffee; it had a dab of white buttercream resting on top.

"I had a little extra batter, but shhhh," Bobby said, creeping closer. "No peeps out of you."

"Thank you," I whispered as my mouth began to water. Treats like this were rare for any of us. We normally ate a vitamin-filled, oat-mealy substance called Vita-Health-Oats. Bobby liked to call it gruel because it was thick and grainy and tasted like nothing. Lick the air and multiply the weight by a thousand—that's gruel. "Did you want some?"

Bobby glanced at the tiny cupcake and then back up at me. "Nah."

"You sure?" I said, almost seeing a flicker of craving in his chocolate brown eyes.

"Baze, how do you think I keep this excellent physique?" Bobby said, taking a step back and flexing his barely discernible muscles.

"Trying to make the cover of a magazine?" Erin laughed from the pantry doorframe. Erin was still in his gray sweats and white t-shirt, the uniform pajamas he always wore to bed.

"Mighty Man," Bobby laughed flexing again.

"Magazine?" I asked.

"Before your time," Erin said, then smirked at Bobby. "I don't think a little cupcake will mess any of that up." He pointed at one of Bobby's arms and chuckled.

"Ha ha. At least I have youth on my side."

"Yeah, that's a good argument," Erin said, pulling out a mug and pouring himself some coffee. If he disliked the coffee as much as I did, he didn't let on. He strolled over to the stove and lifted up the lid of the large pot.

"Is the Vita-Health-Oats done?"

"No," Bobby said, throwing down his hands on the countertop.

"It looks done to me." Erin picked up the spoon and stirred it.

"Yes, it's done, but no it's not called Vita-Health-Oats." Bobby said the name as if it left a bad taste in his mouth. "It is called gruel," he said in a deep Scottish accent, "and you have to say it like that, too. Gruel."

"You can call it whatever you want, Bobby," Erin said. "I'm calling it by its name."

"We've been through this," Bobby countered.

I drifted away from their conversation as I ogled at the cupcake, pulling my attention to the thick buttercream and spongy cake. I took a bite, and it tasted so much better than it appeared. I smiled as I took another bite, feeling as if I'd won some kind of prize. The spontaneous treat reminded me of when Erin and Madam had first found me and pulled me into the kitchen, shivering and shaking with hypothermia. Erin had sat me down on a stool and told Bobby to watch me as they both rushed around the manor for supplies. As Bobby peeked out from behind the refrigerator door, his eyes widened with amazement. It had been years since he'd seen a kid around, let alone one sitting right in front of him.

Uncontrollable tremors had racked my muscles, making me clench my teeth and curl my toes. Bobby just stared at me for the longest time. All of a sudden, his chocolate eyes seemed to turn hazel as a spark ignited in them. He disappeared inside the pantry. A few seconds later, he came strutting out with an armload of ingredients. Bobby began creating something, moving with this elegant fluidity, something I grew up loving. I could tell, even at that young age, he belonged in the kitchen. Before I realized it, a mugful of liquid chocolate rested in front of me. He gave the delightful drink a couple of stirs.

I hadn't fully understood the gesture at the time. What a treat it had been and how expensive the ingredients must have been. I'd sat there quivering, trying to reach for the cup that smelled like safety. Bobby was always sweet that way. He was the one that had taught me that a good sourdough loaf crackles as you pull it from the oven, to always cut away from yourself, to whisper with cake and shout with bread, and that true chefs are always covered in flour and never use measuring cups. He'd also given me my name when I'd realized that, too, rested at the bottom of the swamp.

"So am I going to get my sous-chef today?" Bobby asked, shaking me back into the present.

"Not a chance," Erin said.

"Yeah, I figured you were going to steal her away from me. But look at those big green eyes," Bobby said, pointing at me.

My eyes grew wide as they both turned their heads toward me in unison.

"They're saying—" Bobby's voice came out in a feminine pitch as he crouched down closer to me. "'Bobby, I want to stay and help you with your orders. Don't make me go out with awful Erin.'" He stood up and cleared his throat. "See? The green eyes have spoken."

"I think you're losing it, Bobby," Erin chuckled. "Basil's with me, and that's just the way it is."

"Okay, okay." Bobby shook his head and put his hand on his chest in mocking distress. "It just hurts is all."

"You're young, Bobby. You'll live," Erin said, taking a seat next to me.

"No, Basil is young and kickin'. I'm old and decrepit." His chocolate brown eyes drooped, and his shoulders sagged.

Erin chuckled. "What happened to 'at least I have youth on my side?'"

"Please. You know I only say those things to build up my own self-esteem."

"So if you're old and decrepit at the age of 39, what does that mean for a 53-year-old man?"

"Well..." Bobby tapped his fingers against his chin and sipped his coffee as a stall tactic. He winched as he choked down his horrible concoction. "Well, being that you're the person who supplies Basil and me with decent coffee, I decline to answer."

"Smart move, chef extraordinaire." Erin laughed and gulped down the rest of his coffee.

Erin got up and filled his mug again. Bobby held out his mug to him, and Erin shook his head as he grabbed the almost empty carafe of coffee.

"That's plenty," Bobby said, whipping his mug away. A gulp of coffee splattered onto the tile floor.

"You want coffee with your cream?" Erin joked as Bobby filled his mug with twice as much of it as the coffee.

"Ha ha. Now, Basil, did I ever tell you that you can tell a lot about a person just by what kind of coffee they drink?" Bobby said, stepping over the spilled coffee on the floor.

"No," I said.

"Well, people that like their coffee black are strong, dependable, and most importantly, they don't play games. If they like a little bit of cream and sugar—" Bobby gave me a wink. "—they are sweet and intriguing."

"Okay, kid, what about those that like tons of cream and a dribble of coffee?" Erin questioned.

"They're complex and multifaceted."

"Ha! I believed you up until that," Erin said with deep, full laughs. "Multifaceted."

"What about people that don't like coffee at all?" I asked.

Bobby set his mug down and placed his palms on the countertop. "Run."

Erin laughed, grabbing four bowls and slopping globs of gruel into them. Madam marched into the kitchen through the main swinging door. She leered at the three of us slurping coffee as if we were employees who needed to get back to work.

Erin held up his cup. "Hey, Maggie, come have a cup o' Joe with us."

"I don't drink coffee. You know that, Erin." Her voice held its usual stern reediness to it as she crossed her arms over her chest.

Erin and Bobby busted into a fit of laughter. Erin laughed so hard he started to slap his knee. Bobby's laughs faded into silent gasps of air. Both doubled over, making running gestures while only getting the "r" sound out. Coffee jumped out of their mugs and splattered onto the floor. Their laugher reached my lips, making one corner hike up toward the ceiling.

"What are you still doing here?" Madam glanced at me; her salt and peppered hair was tucked tightly behind her ears.

"I was just getting breakfast, Madam," I said, looking down at the black-and-white tiled floor.

"Don't get mad at the kid, Maggs. We're just having a little fun," Erin said as his pale blue eyes beamed brightly.

"It's the second Tuesday of the month, Erin," Madam jeered, knitting her eyebrows together and making her eyes a harsher blue than normal.

"Oh," Erin grumbled, rubbing his scruffy chin. "Well, Basil's gonna be with me out in the woods setting up rain catchers."

"Okay. You guys have half an hour," Madam said and stormed out of the room.

"You heard the boss. Baze, get dressed and meet me out in the shed."

"Okay," I said and jumped up off the stool.

Three

After I pulled on a pair of well-worn jeans, a hand-me-down gray t-shirt, and a black hooded sweater, I headed down through the kitchen and out the mudroom. As I sauntered through the backyard, the smell of catcher season called out to me. I gazed at the willow trees that sat at the edge of the yard like a giant, living gate. The willows' long branches swayed in the easy breeze.

Behind the willow trees sat a massive forest, one that consumed everything that was neglected, which seemed to be the whole territory. It was like a slow-moving virus, infecting a little more every time I went out somewhere with Erin. It covered condemned houses, abandoned shops, and old, forgotten playgrounds. Erin said that after most people left the territory, the forest took over in their absence. The forest was a beautiful, untamable mess.

I walked to the small wooden shed off to the side of the yard. The shed looked like it had exhaled, because the wood sagged slightly in the roof and walls. The rusted metal hinges whined loudly as I opened the door and stepped inside. Erin was sitting at his desk with his face pushed up against his magnifying glass. He was slumped over his desk, pushing and pulling a needle and thread through one of the tarps. He clutched his hand torch between his teeth. The tarps were a rough, manufactured fabric—a cross between canvas and some synthetic material—making them nearly indestructible. When the tarps ripped, which had been happening more and more due to age, Erin had to sew them up with special thread and seal them with heat.

"Hey there," Erin said without looking at me.

I smiled. "Hi."

Erin cut the thread and sat up as he gave the small patch a few blasts of heat from his hand torch.

"Is that the last one?" I asked, pulling out one of the carts.

"No, I have one more tarp that needs repairs," Erin said, rubbing his eyes as he got to his feet.

He grasped an armload of tarps from a shelf and took them to the decon machine, which resembled a miniature vault. Decon was short for decontamination machine, and it did exactly that—sterilized the tarps to make sure the rainwater stayed pure. Even with the precaution of the decon machine and the electrical grid attached to each opening of the rain catchers, Erin still ran tests to make sure the water was safe to drink.

A long time ago, even before Erin and Madam were born, water sources had started to become toxic due to neglect. There used to be plumbing that brought filtered water through pipework underground, but they'd started to rust and rot away. Madam's parents, Madeline and Hobart Wardell, were one of the first to start catching rain, because when the rain evaporated it was naturally cleansed. Erin met Madam after Hobart hired him for help. He said as soon as he saw Madam, he wasn't exactly in love, but somewhere in that ballpark. Shortly after Erin and Madam were married, Hobart passed away, and Erin took over the business. Madeline fell ill a year later. She'd been bedridden for as long as I'd been around. I'd only seen her a few times when Madam needed help cleaning her bedroom or taking care of her. A couple of times Madam had thrown me into her room with only the protection of a book. On those days, I read to her for hours. I was barred from a certain wing of the manor. Madeline's room rested within that area, as did Bobby's and his wife Lindy's room. Lindy was very sick as well, but from time to time, Bobby would tell me stories about her. I felt like I knew her somewhat because Bobby was such a good storyteller.

After loading up the two carts with tarps and cables, Erin and I trekked out to the catching field. It was a small hike from where we'd set up the initial rain catcher; the one for the Manor was the closest and was always set up first.

"Why can't I be at the manor on the second Tuesday of every month?" I asked Erin as we each lugged a cart of catching gear through the forest.

"You know Maggs. She's gotta have her way with things."

"But why?"

"It's just the way it is, Basil." Erin veered his gaze away from me and steered the conversation in another direction. "It should only take us a week or so to set up all the catchers. Now, do you want to take the left side of the field and I'll take the right?" He asked as we plodded into the archers of open space for the fifty rain catchers we needed to put up.

"We're splitting up?" I asked, excitement leaping in my voice.

He tapped his chin with his index finger thoughtfully. "Seems to me you're well on your way to becoming proficient in the art of rain catching. I'll meet up with you for lunch." He poked my nose before he headed toward his side of the field.

As I hauled my cart to the edge of the field, elation swelled inside my chest and practically popped my lungs. I had never felt so trusted and so well transplanted inside this family than I did at that moment. It didn't matter that I wasn't biologically related to them. I fit all the same. I took a satisfied breath and peered up at the sky. The early morning streaked across it, fuchsia, ginger, eggshell, and a touch of powder blue, seeming to match the way I felt. It was beautiful and picturesque, but I hoped the sky would get murky before the end of the day.

I pulled out a tarp and yanked out a unit of cables, then wandered up to the first set of catcher poles and started weaving the cords through the metal rings.

Four

The morning had soon melted into afternoon, and with it the sun hid behind dark, rumbling clouds. It was coming close to break for lunch, and I had already set up a handful of rain catchers. I finished anchoring down a cord with a knot and began to climb another pole with less vigor than before, exhaustion making my legs feel like the air had turned to water. I stabilized my footing on the small metal platform and rested for a minute before pulling the cable through the thick, metallic ring.

I tugged the cable, throwing all my weight into it to make sure the tarp was set tight before I shimmied down. Suddenly, I was hit by an odd wave of vertigo. The cables and pole spun and whirled, and my head felt feathery light. I managed to grip the wooden pole before toppling off the platform. After what felt like forever, the spinning slowly dissipated, leaving me with a headache in my temples. I took a couple of deep breaths and started gradually making my way down.

Suddenly, my etching felt as if it had burst into a searing inferno. I gripped the cable tighter in one hand as the other became useless as it burned in the invisible flames. The sensation soon devoured my whole arm, raced up my neck, and made my small headache ignite like a supernova. White lights exploded behind my eyelids, turning my muscles to water. I lost my grip on the cable and pole, and the air rushed past my limbs as I plummeted toward the dirt below.

*

I awoke choking on my own fear. My breaths came in wheezing gasps as I lay helpless, sandwiched between leaves and blinding white agony. Minutes turned to years. Finally, my skull extinguished itself and my breaths came more easily. My head felt like a mixture of pain and panic.

"Er—in." His name fractured as it left my lips and saturated the leafy earth under me.

My whole body throbbed and howled with pain, hurting in places I didn't know existed. Two sharp breaths later, I flopped onto my elbow and struggled to heave my upper body up off the ground. My face felt slick with a warm, runny substance. I tried to wipe it away, but as I moved my arm, a jolt shot through it. I gazed down to find that my arm didn't align right; it looked skewed and cockeyed. Half of it went one direction and the other went the opposite way. Panic became a large lump in my throat, and fear rattled through my bones. My mind felt far away. The world around me was somber and abstract in a nightmarish way. I pulled myself up off the ground and staggered through the woods on a set of legs that felt more like string cheese than actual body parts.

"Errrinnn," I stuttered, stumbling over myself. "Hel—help me." As my lips formed around the words, small droplets of panic and fear trickled from my eyes and trailed down my cheeks. Soon, the small path of tears turned to a relentless stream as shudders made my lungs burn and my arm pulsate harder.

"Hello?" His voice shot out from the forest, sounding so sweet and so wonderful to my ears.

"Erin," I cried as my legs melted under me and my head dropped into my usable hand.

I heard him push past the brush, pad up to me, and place his hand on my back.

"Hello?" Erin's voice didn't sound like his own; it was too soft and cautious, and his hand felt too hesitant and hot.

"Is everything alright?" This voice was alien, unfamiliar and strange.

Shock forced my head to jerk toward the sound of his words, and I beheld a set of silver eyes that seemed just as stunned and astonished as I was. He wasn't a man or a boy, but somewhere in between. His face was young, touched by the sun, and intriguingly smooth, with only a few wrinkles of history etched into his skin. I'd never seen a boy so close to my age before. The more I stared at him, the more he seemed somewhat familiar, a hazy, barely lucid memory kind of familiar. He seemed more like a character out of a book I'd once read. His hair, a deep oakwood brown, made his eyes look more alien silver than any normal, human color. His dark locks were cut short and reached up toward outer space in a sort of mohawk.

I swatted his hand away, remembering what Madam had told me about people outside the manor. "You do not know what they're up to, so how can you trust them?" And that was the underlining fact of the matter; I didn't know him. So I couldn't trust him.

"It's going to be okay." His eyes were soft and captivating, and his hands lay peaceful and open.

I glanced down at my sweatband, surprised it hadn't been eaten away by flames. My etching still sizzled like a small burning ember, and a thunderstorm had moved into my skull. I kept waiting for one or both to explode again. I pressed two fingers to my temple but pulled them back when they felt wet and slick. Crimson stained my fingertips, as if the dye on my comforter had splattered across me somehow. My brain hurt even more, because I couldn't remember wandering back to the manor and up to my room. Gravity intensified by a thousand cross-stitching weights on my eyelids and appendages. I heard the rustling of leaves and wondered how they had gotten into my bedroom. The boy knelt closer to me, holding out a balled-up clump of fabric. Had he brought them in?

"Hey, hey, stay with me." His voice was sharper but more distant this time. "I'm not going to hurt you."

I tried to pull away from him as his arms entwined around my frame, but then the clouds above became ruthless, wrapping around the sun and blanketing everything in black.

Five

The light danced across my eyelids like licks of fire, making me see red. Leaves and twigs cracked underneath a pair of bulky boots. My ear pressed against a warm, sturdy wall that palpitated anxiously. I cracked my eyes open and saw limbs of trees stretched out as if to take me away while a set of arms proceeded to do it. The arms carried me securely through the ominous terrain, where boulders morphed into beasts and every sound hissed viciously at me. My head was spinning and my stomach felt queasy. I was a prisoner to these solid arms, but I was too far away from myself to feel fear of where they were taking me.

"Wake—" Parts of the calm male voice seeped into my ears while others drifted on the empty space separating me from reality. "Try—stay with m—almost there."

I wanted to reach out and touch his face, to see if he was real or just a fabrication of my mind. My arms wouldn't respond. None of my muscles would. Long, empty branches of the willow tree gate brushed against my body, greeting me to the backyard of the Manor.

*

It felt as if I had only blinked, but when I opened my eyes, I saw the dingy, florescent lights of the kitchen. The unknown boy gazed down at me while calmness painted his face. He set me on the floor of the kitchen, placing me between the stools. When he pushed open the swinging door, I heard a soft rumble that reminded me of the brutish sky. I listened closely, and soon, the rumble took on a more humanistic quality, as if the manor were buzzing and echoing with people. I had to have been dropped into some bizarre, psychedelic dream, because only in that state of mind would there be that many people in the manor. The boy crept back over to me and knelt down.

"Bobby," I whispered, wondering where he was.

"What was that?" the strange boy asked.

I reached up, using all the strength I could muster, and pressed my index finger to his cheek. His skin felt temperate and real. The boy's eyes darted back and forth between my own. I stared back at his extraterrestrial eyes, so silver they almost frightened me. He pulled up the hood of my sweater, tucking my light brown locks into it, and then pulled up his own hood. He picked me up off the ground and pushed through the swinging door.

"Mom?" The male voice vibrated off my ears, sharp and urgent. His arms entwined tightly around me, pulling me closer to his chest.

"Basil!" Madam's voice spiked to a reedy octave of panic.

"You kno—?"

"Yes…she's just—" Her voice was tense as it muted and broke with my wavering consciousness. "Watch—her right now. Bring—this way."

"I think she broke—possibly…"

They quickly carried me up the enormous staircase and took me down the long hallway; we were deep inside the manor. The boy followed Madam across the beige threshold, into the wing of the manor I wasn't allowed to be in. Madam opened the first door past the threshold, and the boy took me inside and placed me on a velvety blue bed.

"I…get my Mom," he said.

In broken bits, I heart Madam say something about giving vaccinations. He must have left, because she called out to him.

"Yes?" he answered.

"Thank you," she said sharply, and then turned away, letting him know she was done with the conversation. The door thudded closed as Madam wiped at something from her eyes.

Ice compressed my throbbing arm. When consciousness slowly dripped back into my brain, the whole room was overwhelmingly bright. Everything seemed to be draped in a hue of fogginess less dreamy than before. I looked down and saw dozens of wires shooting out of me. Panic instantly consumed my lungs and guts. I wanted to ask what was going on, but everything felt too far away—my nerves from my arms, my voice from my lips, and reality from normalcy.

Nothing seemed real, yet it did. I couldn't deny the truth I was seeing: a metallic machine, dozens of wires colored like a solar burst, and plastic tubing strapped to my nose. The loud hum of a motor vibrated off my arm; the smell of pure oxygen mingled with plastic up my nose; and two fingers that belonged to an outsider pressed inside the palm of my hand. This was unbelievably real.

My gaze followed the two fingers up a slender arm, a broad shoulder, and then to that same set of strange eyes. They were stoic and pacified, so much so that they almost radiated solace into me. Soon, the rest of his face filtered in, and it was the space creature from the forest, the boy that wasn't quite a boy anymore. His calm eyes, sharp face, and dark hair all looked so undeniably familiar.

I felt something prick my arm, and the room swayed back and forth. The Martian boy bloated, twisted, and soon melted into the other items of the room. Everything was seeping into one another, and it felt like someone was covering my eyes with a numbing blindfold.

Six

I felt like I dropped onto a bed from the ceiling as my eyes flickered open. Soft silver and clean plastic drifted from my mind, remnants of a weird dream I couldn't quite remember. I was in my room with my comforter lying awkwardly on top of me. My bed was a calm shoreline, not its usual tsunami aftermath where I was a search-and-rescue worker picking up the pieces. Grabbing my throw blanket, which rested wrinkle-free across the foot of my bed, I headed down the stairs that led into the pantry. It echoed with emptiness, only holding a box of some kind of ingredient for one of Bobby's orders and a sack of dry, uncooked gruel.

As I rounded the corner, Erin came into view, and I couldn't stop myself from colliding into him. His black coffee splashed onto the cream of my blanket, and I glanced down at the red floral stitching and then up into Erin's eyes. His pale baby blues beamed with jubilation. In that moment, a memory of Madam popped into my head. She'd slipped from her usual coarse exterior and revealed to me that the way Erin's eyes lit up was what had made her fall for him and eventually marry him.

"Basil," Erin said with surprise swelling in his voice. "You're up."

Bobby and Madam walked into the kitchen mid-conversation about some order from the upper territories. Their chatter quickly died when they saw me.

Bobby smiled. "Basil."

I smiled back at the two of them as I took a seat on my usual stool. Erin handed me the bowl of gruel that he clutched in his other hand, and Bobby pulled out a mug and filled it with coffee.

"Eat up, kid," Erin said, taking a seat next to me as Bobby placed the coffee in front of me. "We're heading to Gina's today."

Gina was the only mechanic in the territory. Erin usually traded the Bronco for her truck. The truck was massive, able to fit a single car and haul it back to her shop on days she went out to scavenge for them. Erin used her truck on his trips to the Outpost.

"Gina's?" I asked, scooping up a spoonful of gruel. I glanced at the mug of innocent-looking "coffee."

Bobby started pulling out flour, butter, eggs, and other ingredients while Madam fiddled with water order papers. Everything seemed normal but felt strange at the same time.

"Yeah, I'll make today a swap day. Besides, ole Betsy has a cough and needs to see the car doc ASAP," Erin said as he took gulps of his coffee. "Say, you can see your friend Oddy."

My face fell into a grimace before I could stifle my reaction. I quickly wiped the frown from my face and replaced it with a small, content smile. Erin laughed as the conflict inside my head was obvious. Oddy was Gina's daughter, and she was the closest thing I had to an actual friend. Since that she was five years younger and much more happy-go-lucky than I was, however, it was hard to see her in that light.

"What are you up to today, Maggs?" Erin asked.

Madam flipped through the papers, half her attention on the conversation and the other half somewhere else.

"Maggs?"

"What? Oh, just taking care of Madeline," Madam said fixing the order forms in her hands.

Erin rinsed out his mug and placed it in the dish sanitizer. Back at the bar table, he pulled out the ancient map that had been resting on the stool cushion. He unrolled the hand-drawn map and flattened it out on top of the table next to me, placing my mug on one of the corners of the paper to keep it from rolling back up. The map showed our entire territory, number 118. I scanned the map as I had done a thousand times before. I started with Madeline's manor, The Wardell Property written in nice, neat script. Then in Erin's scrawl next to it was, plus Nov occupancy. Erin said he'd added that after Madam had married him, becoming Mrs. Nov. Bobby added plus two McCall boarders later on for himself and Lindy.

I ran my eyes along the thick, tea-colored butcher paper, along miles and miles of wild paper forest. My eyes passed over properties that had been crossed off or marked condemned. I stopped at the little drawing of the Outpost. It was settled inside an old abandoned high school with a small market for food, clothes, gas, and other essentials for barter. There was also a makeshift train station where Erin dropped off Bobby's orders to be sent to upper territories. I'd been there with Erin a few times on his once-a-month trips to replenish our supplies.

"So...Gina's?" Bobby asked.

"Ya, it's about time for a supply run. I'm thinking by the end of this week," said Erin.

My attention drifted back to the manor on the map...actually, to the woods that surrounded the manor. My eyes shifted back and forth methodically, searching for something I wasn't quite sure of. Something didn't feel quite right. I looked up at Erin and Bobby, who were laughing about something they were talking about. I glanced over at Madam and caught her eyes jumping from me back to her stack of papers. I turned my focus back to the paper forest as the odd air in the room made my skin tingle.

"Don't leave me, Maggie," Erin called out to Madam, trying to coax her away from the door. "Aww, stay with me, Maggs."

Stay with me. That phrase rung in my head, covered in a voice I'd never heard before.

All of a sudden, the memory of what had happened the day before rushed back into my brain along with the feeling of fear, the pulsation of my arm, the confusion, the panic, and the pain. Bits and pieces of images engulfed my memory, crashing into one another and against the walls of my skull. Just before I felt completely overloaded, everything hushed as a set of silver eyes consumed all the chaos. I quickly threw off my blanket and examined my arm, the one I remembered dangling like a lifeless animal at my side. I flexed and tensed; it moved effortlessly. Other than a few purplish bruises—which I could've gotten on the catching field—it looked perfectly fine.

"Basil?" Erin asked, taking a step closer to me.

I gawked at the three of them. Madam had wandered toward me; they were unintentionally standing in descending height:

Erin, Bobby, Madam. Bobby was unusually quiet, and Erin peered at me with curiosity deepening the lines around his eyes.

"Where is everybody?" I asked, getting up from my stool. I pushed passed the swinging door and headed down the hallway.

"What are you talking about, Basil?" Erin asked as he followed closely behind.

"The people that were here yesterday," I said, becoming more frantic as I stomped from room to room.

"What?" Erin asked.

"There were so many of them," I said, remembering how their footsteps had sounded like thunder.

"There wasn't anybody but us here yesterday."

I stood in the foyer, staring up at the enormous oakwood doors, seeing the sun's light shimmer off the polish.

"There was a boy," I whispered. "He was my age."

"Basil, you hit your head pretty hard a couple of days ago."

"A couple of days ago?"

"Yes. You're just confused, Baze. It's been only us here, just like always."

I turned around and met Erin's bewildered eyes. Madam and Bobby stood off in the distance, watching me with solemn looks on their faces.

"You know there's nobody your age around here," Erin said. "There hasn't been for over a decade."

"But—" My heart shuddered inside my chest. "But he found me in the forest."

"No." Erin spoke slowly and calmly, the way someone would when trying not to spook someone. "I found you."

"He brought me back here."

"No, I brought you back."

41

"But..." my voice trailed off into nothingness.

I suddenly darted past Erin and launched up the stairs, uncertainty making me crazy.

"Basil! Stop!" Erin shouted, rushing after me.

I ran down the hallway and passed the beige threshold into the forbidden part of the manor, running to the room I remembered being brought into. As my hand curled around the doorknob, Erin's massive mitt of a hand wrapped around my arm and spun me around.

"Basil, stop. What are you doing?" Erin asked, bewilderment seeping further into the creases of his face.

"But... But I remember..." My voice was shaky and confusion felt hot on my cheeks.

"You fell." Erin's eyes were unwavering.

"I... He... I broke my arm."

"No, you hit your head." Erin gripped both of my arms and knelt in front of me, looking into my eyes.

"Please don't tell me I forgot even more," I whispered as tears threatened to spill over the rims of my eyes.

"You took a bad spill is all." Erin wiped at a tear that slipped from my eye. "It happens to the best of us."

"He brought me in here," I said, pointing at the door. "There was a machine and wires and lights."

"I brought you in here. I fixed you up. Basil, feel." Erin brought my hand to my head, and on the side of my forehead was a small gauze pad. "Stitches."

"But I saw it. I know," I said, trying to reach for the doorknob. I took a staggered breath. "I saw him." As the words left my lips, they felt taboo in some way.

"Basil, there's nothin' in that room," he said, shaking his head, his pale blue eyes a gloomy storm of concern.

"There is. It's okay. I know."

"Stop. You don't."

"I do." I tried to reach for the door again, but Erin pinned my arms to my sides. "Please."

Time felt like it passed in hours. Erin took a deep breath and let go of my arms. I grabbed the knob and flung the door open. The room was dark and practically empty. A bed with a blue velvet comforter was neatly arranged with white pillows and a throw blanket. There was nothing else in the room.

Seven

The rain beat hard against the hood of Erin's rickety old Bronco. Normally, we would have been working outside to set up as many rain catchers as possible, especially since it was raining so hard, but Erin said Betsy couldn't hold on much longer and that I should take it easy today, anyway. He was afraid to let me out of his sight, I thought. Like I'd manage to hurt myself again.

"Yeah, I think the check engine light means somethin' this time." Erin chuckled and flicked the windshield wipers to a higher setting.

I followed the raindrops with my eyes as they raced down the passenger's side window and melted into the rubber at the bottom. The droplets reminded me of those old monster movies where, somehow, the creature ended up fifty stories tall and started plowing through the city. I'd never seen one, but Bobby acted them out for me, because I'm deprived of good, old-fashioned entertainment. I'd only seen one movie, a musical Erin kept stored away and dusted off occasionally.

Even though Bobby loved monster movies, he loved Interweb flicks too. The monster movies were the only things Erin and Bobby agreed on when it came to cinema. Bobby would jabber on nonstop as he flipped his egg whites in the mornings.

One time, Bobby thumped around the kitchen, knocking over plastic storage bins as he tried to mimic the movie creature he was talking about. The raindrops were like that, running down the window, unstoppable. My lips perked up thinking about that day I'd spent as Bobby's sous-chef in his kitchen. I stirred a simmering pot of gruel as Bobby roared and growled like an alien monster. I followed suit with a few soft barks. He trounced around so much that Madam stormed in and scolded Bobby for acting childish. After Madam left, Bobby had a good, long chuckle. He didn't take it personally, because Madam needed to have a sense of order in her life, especially after everything she'd been through. I didn't ask what those things were because of the way Bobby had said the last bit of the sentence, like I would've been encroaching on some unspoken topic.

"There you go," Erin said, eyeing my small smirk. "It's gonna be a good day today. Just don't think about it is all."

I shrugged at his statement and wrapped my arms around my torso, pulling my gray sweater more tightly around me. Guilt and shame vaporized all words from my mouth, leaving my tongue feeling dry. I tried to take Erin's advice since he was always right, but those feelings kept gnawing at me. It was the first time I'd been given any kind of responsibility, and somehow I'd messed it up.

The rocky gravel crunched under the tires as Erin pulled up to Gina's makeshift auto body shop. He honked the horn twice, then held it down for two seconds—the secret Gina honk. A minute or two later, Gina came strutting out, wiping grease from her hands. Her curly black hair was pulled into a ponytail, and her blue jumpsuit was so stained it almost looked black. Gina's midnight skin was caked in oil.

"I figured you were going to show up sooner or later." She smiled as she rested her hand on Betsy's hood in front of my window, not bothered by the rain.

I rolled down the window as Erin shouted, "Did ya miss me?"

"No." Gina laughed sarcastically. "I did, however, miss Basil and Betsy."

Gina pulled me into an awkward hug as she practically yanked me through the window. I tried to hug her back, but with the way I was situated in Gina's grip, I ended up squeezing one of her arms and part of her shoulder.

"Oddy missed you too."

"Why don't you head up to the house and say hi?" Erin said, encouraging me to have some kind of social life.

"Okay," I said, already feeling uncomfortable.

I jumped out of the Bronco and started toward the dirt path that led to Gina's house.

"So what did you do to Betsy now, Erin?" Gina opened up one of her garage doors so Erin could park inside.

The dirt path I followed twisted through a neglected junkyard made up of ownerless cars Gina found and stripped for parts. Their frames lay oxidized and eroded as ivy tangled all around them. Only a small handful of cars had some of their parts left. A few cars near Gina's shop looked like they were possible matches for Betsy if she needed a transplant. I made it out of the junkyard, moseyed up the old creaking wooden deck and knocked on the faded blue door.

"Who is it?" Oddy's preteen chime traveled through the door.

"It's me, Basil," I said.

"What's the password?"

"Password? What password?"

"The password," Oddy said, giggling with delight.

The wind seeped through my sweater, and a cold chill trembled through my body. The clouds were almost empty of water as the rhythmic patter of rain started to slow down.

"Oddy," I pleaded.

"Basil!" Oddy shouted and flung the door open, making me jump.

Oddy was a miniature version of her mother, just as beautiful and excitable as Gina, but more of a girly girl. Her thick curly hair framed her face and magnified her huge brown eyes. Her physique, like her mother's, was slender and leggy. Her skin, a rich mocha color, seemed to radiate a bright cheerfulness.

"I'm sooo happy to see you!" Oddy said, throwing her arms around me and linking them behind my back.

"It's good to see you too." I tugged my arm up to pat her on the back.

She squeezed me tightly, then let go and jumped back. I stepped into the house, and she shut the door behind me.

"Notice anything different about me?" She rocked back and forth on the balls of her heels.

Before I could say anything, Oddy did a dramatic spin that ended in an exaggerated curtsy. She held her curtsy for at least thirty seconds, gripping the fabric of her skirt so I couldn't possibly have failed to notice what she was talking about. She clapped her hands as she jumped up and down.

"Very beautiful," I said gesturing to her faded purple skirt.

"My mom got it for me at the Outpost. And look!" Oddy brushed her hair off to the side to show me the new earrings that matched. "I made them and…" She trailed off, prolonging the last word in an announcer voice. She dipped into a hand-sewn pocket. "I made this for you!" Oddy held out a silver chain. Attached to it was a small translucent crystal in the shape of a droplet.

"Aww, thank you. That was very sweet of you."

"You get it?" She pointed to the little gem. "Cuz you're a rain catcher!"

Oddy beamed with satisfaction, and I couldn't help but smile back. She skipped around me and threw the delicate chain around my neck, clasping it shut before I had a chance to protest. I brushed my hand over the extravagant stone. It made my sweater look like a dishrag. Oddy pranced back around to face me, her giant grin still pinned across her face, making her cheeks look apple big.

"We should play a game, but what game? Hmmm." She paced back and forth, tapping her index finger on her head. "Oh, I got it! Hide and seek."

"Okay." I covered my eyes, knowing I was going to be the one seeking her.

"No peeking." She ran away, but seconds later, I heard her pound her way up the stairs.

She wasn't much of a sitter. The first time we met, I was twelve and she was seven. I had brought a book with me to read to her, thinking all kids were like me. Oddy was a good sport. She sat and suffered quietly. Ten minutes had passed before I realized she was bored out of her mind and resorted to making pictures out of the divots in the wall. The manor was mellow, but Gina's was not. I felt like a fish thrown into a different aquarium, one that was filled with fish who didn't breath through gills. I felt bad that I couldn't get comfortable with Oddy. The more I tried, the more awkward I would become.

We played hide and seek for several hours before Erin and Gina wandered into the house.

"You take care of Betsy, ya hear. Old gal has lived a long and beautiful life so far," Erin said.

"If Betsy croaks, it's not because of me," Gina joked. "Now that I got her running smooth again, she'll be fine."

"Okay. Well, let's hit the road Basil," he said waving me to follow.

Gina and Oddy followed us back to the garage. They each gave Erin and I a vise hug, and then sent us on our way.

Eight

The dining room was silent as everyone ate quiet mouthfuls of gruel. I swished my spoon back and forth, pushing the brownish oatmeal substances from side to side passively.

I glanced over at Bobby, who was somber with a melancholy storm cloud brewing overhead. He was in his element in the kitchen, surrounded by loud clanking pots and pans, large appliances, and dozens of timers calling for his attention. Pull Bobby out of all that, and he was sucked dry, transformed into a noiseless man with sadness and gloom pulling his cheeks down.

Madam and Erin were perfectly at peace in the quiet. Erin was like a balloon. At the beginning of the day, he was full of vim and vigor, shooting straight toward the sky, but by the end of the day, he was a deflated piece of rubber. Madam was usually set on her default mode during the day, stern and serious. Now that it was dinner, they both sat tranquilly with their hands entwined in each other's.

"Library for studies," Madam said, patting her clean face with her napkin.

"Okay," I said, fighting the yawn that suddenly crept to the back of my mouth.

"Aww, Maggs, can't it wait till tomorrow?" Erin chimed in. "The kid did just wake up from a two-day coma."

My back felt stiff as my head shifted to my half-eaten bowl of gruel. I took a spoonful and swallowed it hard. It slid down my esophagus in a rough, scratchy way. I wanted to cough, but I didn't want to interrupt.

"And that just supports my argument, Erin." Madam crossed her arms, not in a mean way, but in a businesslike way. "Basil can't fall behind."

The expression she wore was that of a professional educator. It pulled me back into a memory of when she'd first become my professor. Madam was stacking textbooks in front of me, saying, "We cannot have you turn into a wild vagabond roaming around illiterate."

If I wasn't with Madam or cleaning the manor, I was either helping Bobby in the kitchen or out in the forest with Erin. I was always doing something and being watched over by someone. I could probably count on one hand the times I'd been left alone to do whatever I wanted. It didn't bother me; I was sort of used to it.

"Maggs." Erin huffed and gazed straight into her eyes.

A few seconds passed before Madam threw up her hands. "Oh, all right. But tomorrow, after two guys are done setting up your rain catchers, Basil's mine."

"Thank you, my love," Erin said, kissing the top of her hand sweetly.

A hint of a smile played on Madam's lips. Erin had this way with Madam that no one else could touch, and that was just a taste of how he did it. Madam picked up our plates and headed into the kitchen.

Erin grinned triumphantly. "You're off the hook, kid."

"Thanks," I said, getting up from my chair, "and goodnight."

"Already going to hit the hay?" Erin asked. "The night is young, and so are you."

"I'm tired. Probably from—" I hesitated, biting my lip, and then pointed to my head, unable to form the words with my mouth. "—everything, you know?"

Erin nodded knowingly. "Okay. Sleep tight, and don't let the bed bugs have a party in your room without you, 'kay?"

"Okay."

Nine

"Shh, you're safe now."

"Run!"

My feet melted into the ground as mud squished between my toes. My heart thudded in my chest as my legs pushed my body forward. Branches smacked my arms, and foliage bit at my bare feet. Suddenly, I tripped and began to tumble down, falling into a pool of cold, gooey liquid. Panic consumed me. I was trapped and sinking. I fought against the cold swamp that was sucking me under. I wanted to scream, but my throat felt clogged with mud.

I woke to my arms and legs thrashing against my bed, trying to fight their way out of the comforter. My heart thudded in my ears as I pushed my crimson comforter away. I lay there for a handful of panicked heartbeats, then sat up, curling my legs into my chest. The room was bright with the moon's light, and rain tapped my window methodically. I grabbed my throw blanket and headed downstairs. The kitchen was brightly lit with florescent lights casting a hue of yellow over everything.

"You're up awfully late...or early. Whichever way you want to look at it," Bobby said, picking up a disc of dough and smashing it into a ball.

I shrugged and took a seat on my usual stool.

"Can't sleep?" Bobby asked as he started to knead the dough.

"Ya," I whispered, nodding my head.

"Me neither." He slapped the dough down flat again. "So what's keeping you up?"

A chill ran down my spine as I thought of my nightmare—the cold snaking all around me, the fear filling my lungs, the dark. I pulled my throw blanket closer to my chest.

"What are you making?" I asked, trying to change the subject.

Bobby gave a mischievous smile as he leaned into his dough.

"Only the most wonderful and delectable-tasting thing in the whole world."

"Is it a pie?" I asked, peeking around the kitchen to see if I could spot his pie dish.

"Pie? Pie!" Bobby burst into a fit of laughter as he slapped his rolling pin against the counter. "Pie. Please."

"Then what is it?" I asked, not even trying to fight the smile that spread across my lips.

"They're sweet morsels of delightfulness."

"Cookies?"

"Some may call them that."

"You're making cookies?"

"Well, yes, Erin," Bobby said wryly, teasing me for my practicality. "If you want to be all plain Jane about it, they are cookies."

"Mmmm."

"Cookies are the forgotten delicacy of desserts. You know, the last time I made these particular cookies was right before Lindy and I moved here. We had been married four years, and it was late and dark like it is right now. It was snowing, too," Bobby said, throwing flour into the air. "Lindy had just come home from another long day at the health clinic. She walked up behind me and gripped my shoulders." Bobby mimicked the movement, grabbing at air. "'Let's move,' she said, just out of the blue, while I was wielding a cookie cutter, no less."

Bobby pranced over to the drawer next to the oven and pulled out a star cookie cutter. He twirled it around his index finger as he strutted back up to me.

"Whoa!" Bobby shouted as he threw the cookie cutter some more flour into the air. "Lindy, you gotta warn a guy before you drop a jelly doughnut of a bomb like that." Bobby said, looking behind him as if he were talking to her. He then took a step back and mimicked Lindy's voice. "There is a position open in territory 118 for a live-in nurse for Madeline Wardell. Can we please go?" He stepped forward again and sniffed the air dramatically. "They're burning! They're burning! My babies!" Bobby slunk over to the oven and pulled out an imaginary tray of cookies. "Oh no!" He smacked his flour-covered hand against his head. "They're burnt."

I scooted closer to the edge of my stool and planted my elbows on the bar table, resting my head on top of my palms.

"I burned the cookies, Lindy." Bobby sauntered up to the bar table and held his hands out as if he were planting them on Lindy's shoulders. "I'll be laughed out of the bakery if anyone finds out about this. I guess we have to leave now." Bobby shifted to Lindy's spot, clearing his throat and saying in a high falsetto note, "Your secret's safe with me, Robert. Thank you."

I clapped my hands as Bobby ended with a bow.

"Thank you. Thank you. I'll be here all night. The truth is I saw that coming. I was just waiting for Lindy to tell me herself. Hey, it's me; I'm always up for a new adventure." He winked. "Besides, if we hadn't moved to the manor, I wouldn't have been able to wow Erin with my astounding culinary masterpieces," Bobby said, planting his fists on his hips and puffing up his chest.

"Whoa there, kid." Erin laughed from behind me. "Take it down a notch. You might have a hard time cooking if your head gets any bigger."

"Oh, don't deny it. Basil and I both know how much sweeter I made your life, right, Baze?"

I gave a small nod.

"See?" Bobby said as he flattened his dough with the rolling pin.

"Whatever, kid."

"I win!" Bobby cheered as he threw up his hands.

"Okay, okay." Erin pulled out a mug and filled it with water. "Everyone should head back to bed." He handed me the mug and nudged me off the stool, and I headed back upstairs, grinning softly.

Ten

I peered out of the old, cloudy window of the shed to see the morning sun slowly peeking up from the tips of the trees. Everything was glazed in fresh, chilly frost, dazzling like iridescent gems in the dawn's light. I adjusted my dark green sweatband, purely out of habit, and then turned my attention to the dusty insides of the shed. The mustard-colored plastic containers were neatly assembled together, each stacked inside one another. I ran my fingers over the last large stack of tarps when Erin grunted his way into the shed.

"Two days, I'm thinkin'," he said, rubbing his fingers against his chin.

"We'll be up and running in no time." I smiled up at him.

Erin threw an armload of tarps into the decon machine and turned it on. I followed him to the racks of cable units and grabbed as many as I could carry. We loaded the two carts with gear. One was full of cables and the other was full of tarps, which meant we weren't splitting up. My heart sank a little inside my chest at that realization.

"Okay, kid. Let's head out," Erin said as he snatched the last batch of tarps from the decon machine.

We trekked into the catching field, stopping at an empty set of poles; Erin pulled out a tarp as I seized a unit of cables, and we began to weed the cords through the rings at the top of the tarp. When we finished, Erin shimmied up the first pole, and I did the second pole. We moved soundlessly, alternating between poles, and before long the rain catcher was operational. The rest of the day went as smoothly and noiselessly as that.

We trudged into the manor later that afternoon, covered in mud and exhaustion. Bobby was flying around from the countertop to the stove, to the refrigerator, and back to the countertop like a constructive hurricane.

"I'm almost done with my orders," Bobby said victoriously as he whipped a bowl of batter.

"You got one more day," Erin said as he grabbed a ceramic cup and filled it with water. "Then, I'm heading to the outpost early the day after tomorrow."

"I'll make it. I'll make it," Bobby chanted. "I always think I won't make it, but, ha-ha, I always do."

"You can do it, Bobby," I cheered.

"Before long, your gourmet creations will be on a train heading for the upper territories." Erin grinned, handing me the cup of water.

"Yeah, where they'll sit on a quaint shelf and double in price." Bobby coughed out a laugh.

Some of Bobby's creations were sold in territories where people still used currency. I was handing the cup back to Erin when Madam strutted in.

"Basil, make sure you wash up before we start your studies. You have fifteen minutes to meet me in the library," Madam said as she headed out of the kitchen as quickly as she'd come in.

Bobby gave me a bowl of gruel as Erin handed me a bucket of water. Bobby gave me a bowl of gruel as Erin handed me a bucket of water.

Hours later, after I was thoroughly scrubbed and had spent what seemed like a lifetime with Madam and her textbooks, it was time for dinner.

"There is something different about this meal," Erin said, taking another spoonful of gruel.

"Yeah, I taste it too," I agreed.

The gruel actually tasted like something; it was sweet with a hint of spice. I looked over at Bobby to see if his face was beaming with playful mischief, but his lips were in their usual stooped frown.

"I had extra spices," Bobby said, letting gruel fall from his spoon and back into his bowl. "I added them."

"Well, this is really good, Bobby," I said my grin widened.

"Yeah, thanks for the treat," Erin added.

"Thank you, Robert," Madam said but suddenly placed her hand over her lips. Her eyes became mournful. "I'm sorry."

When I looked over at Bobby, his spoon had frozen in midair and his eyes were glazed over. He dropped his spoon and dropped his face into his hands. After minutes of agonizing motionlessness, Bobby stood up and meandered out of the room. Robert was what Lindy had always called him. I wondered if hearing other people say it reminded him that his wife was sick, that she hadn't been the same in quite some time.

Maybe he could really only hear it from her lips, with her voice coating it in sweetness.

The rest of dinner passed without another word. I met Madam in the library for several more hours of studying. By the time I made it into my room, the moon spilled in through my bare window, drenching my bed in its light. I dropped onto my mattress, ready for delightful sleep to tuck me in and my feathery pillows to say goodnight.

Eleven

The next day passed without unpredictability, and so the rain catchers were all set up, and Bobby was in the midst of completing all his orders. After dinner, which was sandwiched as usual between my study sessions, I headed up to my bedroom. I changed into my pajamas and fell onto the bed in my typical exhausted way, curling under my marshmallow covers and pulling my downy pillows closer to me as sleep prepared to swallow me whole.

*

The sensation of fire eating at my arm woke me from my slumber. The stark, dark night had turned my room black, and the moody sky beat a heavy rain against my window. My fingers twisted in the sheet as the flames clawed up my arm and devoured the side of my neck. The sensation moved to my cheek and scorched it, but the burning was faintly stifled as a nuclear bomb detonated inside my head. I jerked so hard from the blast in my brain that I dropped onto the hardwood floor. I whimpered as my body began to warp from the pain, legs twitching and coiling tighter around my comforter as my hands gripped my screaming head.

Everything felt so horribly and sickeningly hot against my skin. I yanked my blanket away and pushed aside the pillows that had tumbled down with me. The heat still ate at me feverishly, so I yanked off my sweater and pressed my searing cheek onto the coolness of the wooden floor. The hotness spread to my stomach, churning the gruel that rested inside. I wrenched myself up off the floor and stumbled to the washroom gracelessly.

I didn't even have time to flick on the light switch before my innards charged up my throat and flooded my mouth. I crumpled to the ground, grabbing the empty bucket that rested next to the old porcelain toilet. Hanging my head over the bucket, I heaved up my insides in intervals. My body jerked and cringed revoltingly. My world felt unstable as my limbs trembled and shook with something other than fear. I clutched the plastic bucket as if holding it could somehow hold the world still.

After the dry heaves stopped, I wiped my face with a small hand towel. Something inside of me was strangely and terribly wrong. The heat from my etching still ate at me, but in a less intense way, a way that gave me access to my brain. I glared at my sweatband, able to make out its dark shape against the paleness of my skin.

For the first time in my life, I wanted the etching to disappear. I wanted it off me. I wanted whatever it was to be gone. My stomach stirred unnaturally, and my etching started to heat up angrily as if it had heard me somehow. Using the sink, I was able to hoist myself onto my feet. Even in the blackness, I could make out my silhouette in the mirror. I wanted this to stop. I want to be normal. I wanted everything to be and feel like the way it used to.

The fury bubbled underneath my skin, pushing against my etching. I was so livid that I ripped off the sweatband and threw it as far away from myself as possible, as if I could get rid of the etching on my arm that easily. As the absorbent band smacked against the mirror, the washroom became engulfed in a vivid fluorescent light. I looked down at my forearm. The usual deep lines of scar tissue were now lines of glowing yellow-gold. The light was emanating from underneath my skin!

My breath caught in my throat in a choking, suffocating way. The room suddenly grew darker, eerier. I pressed the palm of my hand to my chest, trying to make my windpipe open, but my terror kept my lungs deprived of air. My eyes were glued to the glowing light that poured out of me and stained the walls with gold. My surroundings became ever more unstable as the edges of it grew darker. My world became a shattered snow globe, broken puzzle pieces falling apart and away from me. Everything broke down into flecks of dirt and ash; light was dark, up was down, tile was ceiling, and gold seeped through all the holes in between.

I took in short, staggered breaths as if the bizarre glow had pushed all the air out of the room faster than I could draw it in. My heart hammered rapidly, and the burning liquified my muscles. I fell onto my knees, feeling my etching slowly infect my body and push away my consciousness. There was no escaping this nightmare. Everything was fleeing away from me, and I couldn't fight the blackness. As black and yellow consumed me, all I heard was the rattling of rain against wood. Soon, the gold melted into black completely, and the beating rain took my escaping consciousness into a memory I had long forgotten.

*

I stared at the tarnished gold lamp that sat on a white table; the table was so old that the paint was curling and flaking away from the wood. The room was dark, and the night rumbled anxiously outside. I was wearing clothes Madam had brought me. They hung big and baggy off my frame. Everything felt new and strange—I didn't know or trust anyone.

"You can't say anything," Erin said harshly to a woman with fiery copper hair. They were standing just outside the sitting room.

"What's going on, Erin?" the woman asked.

"Shh, Erin. She's right there," Madam said, then started to pad toward me.

"What?" asked the woman with copper hair. "She?"

She and Erin followed Madam into the living room. The woman's eyes grew wide as she spotted me curled up on the armchair in the corner.

"Oh, hello. My name is Dr. Hofflin," she said as she took tentative steps toward me.

"We found her the day before yesterday," Erin said.

Dr. Hofflin knelt in front of me. Her smile reached her eyes. "What's your name?" she asked, her voice smooth and calm.

I looked back and forth among their faces, fear making me curl my legs into my chest.

"She hasn't said a word to us," Madam said.

Suddenly, a banging noise came from a door outside the sitting room, making me jump.

"I'll see who it is," Madam said, getting up and walking out to the front entrance of the Manor.

"Shhh, it's okay," Erin said as he reached for me.

When his fingertips touched my skin, I jerked my arm away as if they were made of hot coals.

"No! Let us in!" a man with a brutish voice shouted.

"Get out!" Madam yelled as the two men marched into the sitting room.

They spotted Dr. Hofflin and Erin before their eyes zeroed in on me.

"Oh, my goodness. It's true," gasped a small-statured man in a soft voice.

"It's true!" the taller man with the harsh voice spat out.

Erin quickly scooped me up and hurried out of the room. The two men stared at me with wide, astonished eyes as I passed them. Erin took me into the closest bedroom and settled me on top of a cozy bed, wrapping me inside a white throw blanket.

"Get some sleep," Erin whispered and left the room.

I pulled the covers tighter around myself as I strolled over to the door. The murmurs were almost audible. After gnawing on my lower lip for a few tentative and nervous heartbeats, I pressed my ear to the door.

"From what I could tell, Madam," Dr. Hofflin said, "she's roughly nine years ol—"

"You need to get rid of her," the man with the gruff voice stated bluntly.

"What?!" Madam practically shouted.

"It's not safe and you know it."

"Mr. Dervin!" Dr. Hofflin shouted in protest. "You—"

"I get what you're saying, Joe," Erin cut in with a smooth, coaxing voice, "but the honest truth is there's no safer place for her at the moment."

"What?" Joe sounded bemused. "I'm not talking about her safety. I'm talking about yours, about your wife's. I'm talking about my family, George's family. Heck, you might as well throw Dr. Hofflin here and your chef in with that."

"Joe, really?" Erin said as if Joe were a salesperson with a poor pitch.

"Yes, really, or have you forgotten what's happened around here?" Joe's voice was tainted with the harsh sting of anger. "We don't know where she's from or who has seen her. Have you checked her arm? Has she been etched?"

"She's just a little girl. What do you propose we do with her?" Dr. Hofflin said, disbelief clouding her words.

"Put her on a train and send her anywhere but here," Joe said.

"You cannot be serious!" Madam shrieked.

"I am serious, and I'm surprised you're so lighthearted about this whole situation. I thought you of all people would understand!"

A harsh silence fell over the group. It stayed that way for what felt like forever as I went back to chewing on my lower lip. Someone exhaled loudly and started pacing back and forth.

"George?" Erin asked.

"I... I..." the man seemed to be having trouble finding his voice.

"Hello?" the voice of a little boy called out.

I jumped; it had come from within the room. I ripped my ear away from the door and gazed into the shadows.

"Hello?" I whispered.

Footsteps started in my direction, and a silhouette of a small boy came into focus. All of a sudden, something crashed against the ground, and the whole scene began to pull away from me.

From a distance came a voice that didn't belong in the memory. "Basil?"

The room, the tension, the memory all faded away.

"Basil!" Madam's voice made my eyes flutter open.

I looked around and realized I was still on the washroom floor. Dawn had peeked in through the window and lit the room in a cheery light. Madam's sapphire eyes hovered over me as she touched my arm apprehensively.

"What happened?" she asked.

I sat up, pressing the palm of my hand to my head. My brain felt mushy and woozy, and my skin felt hot and cold at the same time.

"Is it your head? Maybe we pushed you too hard too fast," The uncertainty of her voice made her words sound funny; I couldn't remember the last time I'd heard her question herself before.

Madam gripped my arms and helped me to my feet.

"Oh, my," she muttered as she pressed a chilling hand onto my forehead. "You feel a little warm. Are you feeling—" Madam looked at the floor, raised her eyebrows, and then gazed back at me. "—all right?"

"My ar—" My mouth and throat felt dry. I gulped to try to quench their thirst. "My arm."

Madam gaped at my arm, and her eyes grew wide. Her eyes darted around the room frantically.

"Where's your band?"

I glanced at my arm, expecting to the yellow-gold hue, but it looked like it always had, just a slick pink scar. I cupped my hand around my eyes and forearm to see if the light in the room was affecting the visibility somehow. Nothing.

"Basil, what are you doing? Has your head been bothering you?" Madam asked, placing my sweatband back over my etching.

"My arm," I said, holding it out in front of me. "It was glowing."

Madam's eyes narrowed, and for a split second, I thought she believed me. "I think you need some rest," she said instead.

"It was glowing gold."

"I want you to get some rest today."

As Madam pulled me out of the washroom, I noticed that a bucket of cleaning supplies lay tipped over, and bottles were scattered across the hallway floor. Madam was too logical to believe in the impossible, but it was true. I felt it crawling and clawing inside my body; my head still throbbed at the temples from it.

"But—but it started burning last night," I tried to explain.

"I'm sorry, Basil. We should have let you rest more," Madam said, escorting me into my room as if I were five.

The comforter and sheet were twisted and mangled, hanging half off my bed. The pillows lay marooned across my floor. Exhaustion pulled at my arms at the same time Madam's icy hands did.

"Where's Erin?" I asked, knowing I would have a better chance at explaining this to him.

"He's at the Outpost for the day."

Madam stripped my bed of its comforter, leaving my cream-colored sheet and a solitary pillow. She directed me to lie down and guided my head to the pillow. Fatigue added weight to my eyelids, and the soft bed lulled me into an unwanted sleep.

"But Madam—" I whispered.

"I'll be back to check on you," she said as she tucked me in. "Don't bundle up." With that, she marched out of my room.

Twelve

I slept as if I were dead to the world, only rousing for a few seconds at a time as Madam came at me with a glass of water, forcing me to drink. I swallowed water that tasted too cold and fell back into an unthinking stupor where time seemed irrelevant.

I finally regained lasting coherency as the smell of Bobby's coffee wafted into my room, filling my nose with its rich aroma. Wrapping my sheet around my arms, I made my way down the staircase and into the pantry. It was packed full of food; colorful boxes and cans lined the walls from ceiling to floor.

"It will be okay," Erin said calmly.

"I'm worried about her, Erin," Madam whispered. "Maybe, we should have—" she quickly stopped talking as the wood groaned under the weight of my feet.

"Bobby?" Erin called out.

I turned the corner with a small, sheepish smile.

"Good morning, kid." Erin smiled back at me.

He pulled out a stool and patted the seat, inviting me to join him. Madam stood next to the bar table that connected with the countertop. She fidgeted with the stack of papers in her hands. Bobby's coffee smelled slightly burnt, as if it had been sitting for a while.

"How are you feeling?" Erin asked, reaching for a banana that rested in a bowl next to the sink.

"Fine."

He handed me the banana, and Madam placed a glass of water in front of me.

"Thank you," I whispered.

My mouth watered as I broke open the yellow rind and peeled it back. I bit off small pieces, trying to savor each sweet and scrumptious bite. I smiled, grateful that Erin always remembered us whenever he made trips to the outpost.

"So I was going to go to Gina's to drop off her truck," Erin said, taking a swig of his coffee.

Madam nudged the cup of water closer to me; I took several gulps of it between bites. I looked over at the coffee pot, longing for some caffeine but having enough self-control to finish my banana and cup of water first.

"I was wondering if you were up to going with me, Basil."

"Yes, I am."

"Are you sure?" Madam placed her hand onto my forehead.

Erin set a cup of coffee down in front of me and pressed his palm to my forehead as well. He nodded approvingly and moved his hand to my cheek. His eyes grew intense and focused as he ran his finger across the gauze pad taped to the side of my forehead.

"Hold still," he said as he pulled lightly at the tape. After he removed the bandage from my head, he took a second to examine it.

"Gotta love dissolvable stitches," Erin cooed.

I ran my fingers along my forehead and felt a small scar running along the side of my hairline.

He poked my nose with his finger. "I think you'll be all right, kid."

Madam crossed her arms and shook her head disapprovingly; her sapphire eyes hardened with her displeasure, and her lips pressed into a tight line. She tucked her hair securely behind her ears. Her face had its usual seriousness back.

"Don't worry, Maggs, I'll keep her safe." Erin smiled and kissed Madam on her cheek.

Madam conceded, as she touched Erin's chin with slow surrendered fingers. Erin's eyes lit with delight. On her way out, she stopped and moved her arm toward me, but she quickly drew it back as though someone had smacked it. Madam grimaced down at her papers like she had just remembered something vitally important, then marched out of the kitchen.

Thirteen

After loading Gina's truck up with barrels of rainwater—
Erin's payment for her services and truck usage—we headed
off toward her shop. I sat in the passenger's seat and played
with the fuzz on my sweatband, wanting to open up to Erin but
not knowing where to start. Anxiety washed over me, and
soon, I began tracing the patter of my etching with my fingertip
across my band. Erin hummed quietly as he gripped the
steering wheel with one hand. I bit my lip, trying to build up a
reservoir of courage.

"Erin?"

"Basil?"

I glared at my sweatband, keeping all my visual focus on the
fuzz that sprouted out from it.

"I was just wondering," I started, pulling at the fluff again.
"Why do I nee—" I gulped, sipping from my tank of courage.
"—need to cover up my etching?"

Erin took a sharp breath and but exhaled slowly. "Basil, I
thought we talked about this already."

"Do you know why I have it? How did I get it? What is it? Why—"

"Whoa. Whoa. Whoa. Hold on, Basil."

I snapped my mouth shut and laced my fingers together.

"Why the sudden interest?" he asked.

"Well…" I took a hard swallow, telling myself that this was my chance, my chance to explain to Erin what had been going on.

"Because I've told you everything you need to know." His voice was slowly turning to ice. "We found you. Your arm was etched. That's it."

"But why do I have to hide it?"

"You just do, all right?" His face was beginning to look more like Madam's.

"Erin, my etching—"

"Stop!" he shouted, making my heart jump. "Trust me, Basil. You know everything you need to know."

Silence filled the cab of the truck and lingered for a few minutes.

"What does that mean?" I asked shyly.

His exhale was loud and exaggerated, and he gripped the steering wheel with both hands.

"It means I'm trying to protect you, because you don't need to know. Because things can't go back to normal after you find out. Telling you is unnecessary. Once you know, you can't just erase that kind of information. You have no idea–" He stopped abruptly. "It's done. It's over. Neither I nor you can change the past."

Erin pulled into Gina's driveway and set the truck in park. He pressed his fingers to the bridge of his nose, looking like a sad statue. Seconds later, he wiped his eyes with the collar of his shirt, trying to make it seem casual. I'd never seen Erin look so upset before. I pulled down the sleeve of my sweater and covered my sweatband.

"Basil, just know this." He turned toward me. "Everything I do is because I love you, okay?"

"Okay," I whispered, suddenly feeling guilty for bringing it up.

Erin turned back to face the steering wheel and did the secret Gina honk. Gina came sashaying out to greet us and her truck. I gripped my arm apprehensively, trying to hide my shame. If Gina could feel the tension between Erin and me, she didn't let on. She just smiled her bright, beaming smile and patted the hood of her truck peacefully. After a giant, constricting hug, Gina sent me on my way to the house.

I knocked on the door and waited for several minutes before knocking a second time. When several more minutes had passed, I turned the doorknob; it was surprisingly unlocked. I stepped inside and closed the door behind me.

"Oddy?"

I kept waiting for her to jump out from behind a door or trample down the stairs. I scanned the living room, down the hallway, and up the stairs without stepping a foot away from the front door.

"Hello?" I called out again.

I gave up waiting and wandered up the stairs to try her bedroom. Oddy's door was easy to spot due to the faded pieces of colored paper. Most of the papers had pictures of flowers drawn across them, but a few had sentences like Beware of the Oddy Monster or Only Oddies Allowed. I turned the handle and pushed the door open. Inside, Oddy's lean frame was curled up on her bed against the wall.

"Hey, Oddy," I said, sitting down on the corner of her bed.

"Hey," Oddy whispered. She flipped around and tugged the sleeves of her shirt down.

"How's everything?" I asked.

"All right," Oddy said, but she wore her lips in an odd, emotionless line.

"Is there something wrong?" I asked.

I'd never seen her so quiet and devoid of energy before. She balled up the edges of her shirt in her palms and pushed them under her cheek. Her legs were pulled close to her chest. Her enormous, dark brown eyes were full of uncertainty and sadness.

"Umm…no?" she said, staring off into the distance.

"Oddy," I cooed, trying to be as soothing and comforting as Erin usually was. "You can tell me. We're friends." I took a small gulp, but in my heart, I knew it was true. "Right?"

"Yessss." Oddy exhaled slowly, sitting up and pushing the tips of her sleeves together.

"So," I said calmly, "what's going on?"

"Okay." She hesitated for a second or two as she glanced up at me, but then went back to staring at her sleeve-covered hands. "My mom and I were out searching for cars, you know, so when we got the truck back, we would be ready."

"Yes," I said in encouragement.

"We usually split up cuz the junkyards are so big. Well, at the last place we went to, we separated like normal. I was sifting through the piles of trash when there were these men." Oddy twisted her sleeves together nervously. "They were in black pinstriped suits. I'd never seen clothes look so new before. They had leather briefcases, too. They…umm." She looked down at her sleeves again.

"They what?" I asked, trying to stay calm. "What did they want?"

"They wanted to talk to me." She cocked her head to one side. "They knew my name. They knew everything..." She trailed off as she gazed up at the wall, losing her train of thought.

"What did they want to talk to you about?"

"My mom's been struggling with—" Oddy took a deep breath.,"—everything. Did you know that?"

"No."

"Yeah." She was quiet for an unusual amount of time. "I was thinking I should tell my mom about what happened at the junkyard." She blinked up at me, asking with her eyes what I thought.

"I think you should."

I glanced down at her sleeve-covered hands, wanting to know if she was hiding something but at the same time not wanting to know at all.

"Okay. Okay." She nodded.

"Okay," I said.

"So what game do you want to play?" Her smile was forced, and her eyes still looked sad.

"Hide and seek?" I asked.

"Sounds good." She slipped off her bed.

I covered my eyes and started to count.

Fourteen

Betsy rumbled quietly as we traveled along the dirt path that led to home. Erin gripped the steering wheel with one hand. I pressed my head against the window, gazing out at the darkening sky. All of a sudden, Erin pulled Betsy to a stop. My head jerked from the window, and I looked over at Erin. The corners of his lips were raised in a mischievous smile.

"I'm thinkin' you need some drivin' time," he said, rubbing his chin.

I smiled timidly. "Really?"

"Oh, yes. Driving is an essential thing to learn, and you know what Maggie says." He smirked as he straightened his face, trying to act serious. "Essential matters first."

Erin chuckled a little as he reminisced. Madam had used that line several times when Erin or Bobby tried to steal me away from my studies. It'd been a while since she'd said it, probably because they had learned not to ask, but I'll never forget the way one of her eyebrows twitched up as she did. A small smile brushed my lips, fading as quickly as it came; the events of the day seemed to have sucked all the humor out of my body.

Erin scooted out of the driver's seat as I jumped out of the passenger's seat. I forced a smile across my face, which wound up being tight and rigid. Soon, I was behind the wheel and Erin was dozing in and out of sleep. I'd driven the Bronco a handful of times. As the road started to curve, I knew we were getting close to the manor. Betsy shook and rattled as I ran over the dozens of potholes that littered the manor's brick driveway. Erin roused from sleep, stretching out his arms and taking a long, deep yawn. As he rubbed sleep from his eyes, I pulled into the garage. Like everything else in the manor, it was enormous.

"We're alive," said Erin, mocking me playfully.

"Well, everybody knows I'm a better driver than you," I said with a sly smile, but then it dropped and I wanted to retreat.

"Oh, ouch." He laughed and pressed his hand to his heart. "Was that really my little Basil that just said that?"

I gave a small, apologetic smile, but he just kept laughing as he patted my cheek a couple of times and opened his door. I shadowed him as he made his way out of the garage and into the foyer.

"Oh, good. You're back," Madam said from the doorframe of the dining room. "Dinner is ready."

Dinner came and went as it always did, with Madam and Erin tranquil and quiet, Bobby sad and silent, and me reserved and tongue-tied. After dinner, I was quickly whisked away by Madam and taken into the library for my studies. Since dinner had been served earlier than normal, I watched the sand in Madam's hourglass empty three times. My head became a chaotic mess of literature, mathematics, biology, and other

84

subjects that fried brain cells. My forehead hurt from all the information, although lately, the pain in my left temple seemed to be constant. Now it had a friend.

I left the library in my usual sleepy daze and headed up to my room. I changed into my pajamas and flopped onto my mattress, hoping sleep would dull the pulsations in my head. Just before my eyelids fell victim to sleep, a chill traveled through my body, making my covers seem gauzy thin, even though they fluffed up like whipped cream. The cold had finally settled inside the manor; it was well into catcher season. Throwing on a sweater, I trekked down the dark hallway, tripping over my feet lethargically. I was in search of the thick blankets Madam kept stored away in cabinets around the manor. I must have had the thickest skin, because I kept hitting empty cabinets.

I finally managed to find a hefty brown blanket, and as I pulled it out, I realized how far into the manor I was. Staring straight at me was the beige threshold. The prohibited part of the Manor was but five feet away from me. Clutching the blanket closer to my chest, I closed the empty distance and gazed into the vacant hallway that seemed all too innocent. My toes almost touched the edge where the hardwood floor switched from diagonal to vertical.

It seemed forbidden, a line I should never cross. Aside from my most recent crossing, I'd only crossed the threshold once, by accident of course, and regretted it dearly. It was back when I easily got lost inside the manor; I was trying to find a washroom and ended up using one past the threshold. The warning didn't seem so serious to me back then. Madam simply told me not to cross it, her face cold and serious as always. As soon as I exited the washroom, Erin spotted me, his face a mask of anger and horror. He rushed up to me and yanked me downstairs by my arm. He gave me a long, half-yelling lecture. From then on, I knew how I should view that wing of the manor: completely off limits.

I took a step and straddled the threshold, feeling scared, rebellious, nervous, and anxious—a soup of emotions simmering inside my stomach. My unanswered questions seemed to be the spoon that stirred the soup. Those questions pulled at me, making me want to raid the forbidden hallway by opening every door inside of it. I took another step and stood with the boundary line pressing on my heels. The hunger for answers was overpowering.

I gripped the blanket tightly in my hands, feeling deceived, feeling disloyal, so overwhelmingly torn. The part of me that didn't want to believe that I was being lied to, the part that wanted everything to stay the same, pulled me back and away from the threshold. The fragments drifting in my stomach that wanted to believe Erin was right—that the past didn't have anything to do with me now—yanked me safely inside my bedroom. And the pieces inside my heart that wanted to box up the gut-wrenching questions and hide them for another day forced me to close my door and go to bed. I fell into a fitful sleep.

Fifteen

Weeks passed, and things finally felt normal again. Erin and I emptied all the rain catchers into barrels and stacked them inside the shed. While we waited for another big storm, Erin tested the water, and my time was split between cooking with Bobby and cleaning with Madam.

"Okay, sous-chef Buttercream, can you grab me a bag of apples, please?" Bobby said, stirring a simmering pot.

I lugged out a large bag of green apples and gently placed it onto the countertop.

"Come on, Earl, caramelize my sugar nice and pretty," Bobby whispered to the stovetop. "Your mission, should you accept it," he said to me, turning his blue mitten potholder into a puppet, "is to peel apples. This potholder will self-destruct in five seconds."

"All of them?" I asked as I pulled out the peeler.

"Yes, all of them. Boom!" Bobby yelled, throwing the potholder in my face.

We laughed as I peeled the apples, and Bobby turned his attention back to his sugar.

"Aww, so beautiful," Bobby squeaked, pulling the pot off the stove. "It's so perfect."

I peeked inside the pot. "It's gorgeous. You deserve a round of applause," I said, clapping in a circle.

"Thank you. Thank you," Bobby said, taking the pot and beginning to pour the sugar into another bowl that was filled with dry ingredients. "Did I ever tell you about the time I almost gave up trying to be a chef?"

"Yes, but I would love to hear it again." Bobby's stories became more fable-like the more he repeated them.

"Okay, I had been married a year," Bobby started. He usually used pre-Lindy and post-Lindy as his timeline. "Lindy came home, and the whole house was filled with thick, black smoke. I mean, I couldn't see a fork in front of my face. Not a thing!" Bobby said, moving through the kitchen as if he couldn't see anything. "Lindy called out for me, seeming all too happy. 'Robert! Robert!'" Bobby jumped up and down, flicking hair over his shoulder, as if he had long, magnificent locks. "She was always peppy like that, too. 'Robert! Robert!' Lindy was my cheerful little ball of sunshine, always keeping me on my toes." He cleared his throat and straightened his posture. "Yeah, Lindy. I'm here. I pulled the pan out of the oven and started dowsing it with water." Bobby mimicked what it looked like, frantically throwing imaginary water onto an imaginary pan. "We opened up the window to try and clear out all the—"

"Basil." Madam's sharp voice broke into Bobby's story. "Basil, I need your help cleaning the manor." She marched into the kitchen through the swinging door.

"Okay, Madam," I said, setting the apple and the peeler on the counter.

Madam quickly stormed out of the kitchen as I washed apple juice from my hands. I blinked at Bobby with apologetic eyes, but he shrugged and threw up his hands dramatically.

"Duty calls," Bobby said, flashing me one of his dorky grins. "We'll have more fun later."

I nodded as I pushed through the door, disappointed that Bobby couldn't finish his story even though I'd heard it a dozen times. In the midst of his story, Bobby would up onto the countertop, make a handful of funny faces, jump back and forth from being Lindy to being himself, and salsa dance around the kitchen island with a broom. In the end, Lindy would make Bobby open up and tell her what was really going on. Bobby always finished by saying that the moral of the story was to find someone who saw past the façade that fooled everybody else. "You want someone who knows the real you," he'd say.

I smiled quietly to myself, tucking away Bobby's pearls of wisdom, partially thinking I'd have no real use for them but loving their beauty all the same. My mind wandered further than I thought, and I wound up knocking into Madam.

"I'm sorry," I blurted.

"I need you to clean the downstairs," she said, handing me a bucket of cleaning supplies, the grip worn from use. "Whatever you don't finish today, you can do tomorrow. I'll be upstairs." Madam picked up another bucket that looked identical to mine and headed for the stairs.

I grasped the handle of the bucket and headed for the sitting room.

Sixteen

It was day two of my cleaning frenzy, and I had finally gotten into a rhythm: dust, clean windows, scrub floors, and polish. I moved as if Bobby were singing one of his favorite songs. I was in the foyer, picking up the runner and shaking it out like a musician keeping the beat. I rolled up the rug and left it off to the side while I swept. As I cleaned the floor, I occasionally danced with the broom or mop—after making sure I was completely alone, of course.

When I finished the foyer and unfurled the runner where it belonged, I loaded all the cleaning supplies back into the bucket. As I headed to the garage, I heard furious knocking against the door of the main entrance. Instinct made me freeze, transforming me into a rigid statue. The knocking stopped, and silence blared in my ears for a few heart-pounding seconds. Then the knocking turned into pounding.

"It's me, Gina! Open up!" she shouted into the thick oakwood door.

I rushed over to the door and quickly unlocked it. Gina shoved it open, and I jumped out of the path of the door as it flew past me. Her face looked different, cold and empty. It made me think of the last time I'd seen Oddy, and I wondered if she had spoken to Gina.

Before I had time to do anything, she lunged for me, her arms outstretched, reaching for me. I backpedaled, thrusting out my right hand defensively. She gripped my arm like a vise. Her face was twisted with anger, pain, and other indecipherable emotions. I tried to jerk my arm out of her grip, but her hands just tightened against my struggle. I lost my balance and stumbled backward, making the bucket fall from my fingertips. The bottles clattered across the floor as Gina yanked up the sleeve of my sweater. I tripped on one of the bottles and fell into a small table. As I thumped to the ground, I saw Madam's handcrafted—always out but never used—vase tumble off the corner of the tabletop and shatter against the clean, polished floor.

Everything was happening so rapidly. There was no time to scream or run. Somewhere in between the two landings, the vase's and mine, my arm had been released. I frantically scrambled backward on my palms and heels. Gina gripped my left arm and tugged on my sweater.

"Gina!" Bobby's voice shouted in the distance.

The interruption didn't stop her from yanking up my sleeve and ripping off my dark green sweatband. Her breath escaped her mouth as if someone had knocked her in the stomach. She gaped at me, her deep brown eyes wide and heartbroken.

"I knew it." Gina wept as she ran her shaking fingers across my etching. "You did this."

"Gina," Bobby said, pulling her off me.

"You did this!" she screamed, struggling against his grip.

"I'm sorry," I choked out, pushing myself under the little table.

"Oh my goodness!" Madam shouted in shock as she stared down at us from the balcony. She ran down the stairs, her black slacks covered in dirt and her salt and pepper hair tucked behind her ears.

"I trusted you," Gina cried at me, wilting in Bobby's arms.

"I'm sorry," I choked out again.

Madam rushed over and crouched under the table. She pressed her hand to my cheek, demanding my attention, but Gina's distraught brown eyes hypnotized me as fear constricted my throat.

"Basil?" Madam said.

"What did..." I trailed off, unable to get the question to leave my lips.

"Basil," Madam said sternly, pulling my face to hers.

"What did I do?" I asked.

"Basil, are you all right? Are you hurt?"

"No, I'm not hurt."

Madam got up and marched over to Gina, who had melted onto the hardwood floor. Bobby stood by, watching her with attentive eyes. Madam knelt next to Gina and gripped her on the sides of her arms.

"Gina, what's going on?"

"Oddy. She..." Gina trailed off, sobbing.

Madam persisted. "What about Oddy?"

"I trusted you! I didn't want to believe it was true. I didn't take it seriously enough."

"What about Oddy?" Madam asked in her nonnegotiable way.

"They took her," Gina cried. "My baby! My Oddy. They took her!"

Time seemed to have stood still. Gina sobbed so hard she was hyperventilating. They were the type of deep, grieving sobs felt throughout your entire being, ones that pierced your heart.

"Oddy's gone." It wasn't a question, but a statement. It was fact, and fear was laced around her words.

"You brought them here." Gina glared at me, her face streaked with tears. "This is all your fault."

"I'm sorry," I mumbled.

"Bobby, take Basil to her room," Madam ordered.

"I didn't want to see it. I didn't want to believe the stories, but it's there. The etching is right there on her skin."

"Bobby?" Madam hissed, glaring at him until he moved toward me.

Bobby grasped my hand and pulled me onto my feet. He toted me up the stairs with his arm wrapped around my shoulders. I glanced at Gina. She was sobbing, shuddering in Madam's arms.

"What did I do?" I asked.

Bobby didn't say anything to me. He was as quiet as the night, and his face was solemn.. Bobby pushed my door open and led me inside.

"What is going on?" I asked with a little more force behind my words.

"I'll come get you when things calm down," he muttered.

"Bobby?" Tears teetered on the edges of my eyelids.

His eyes were distant, making them a deep, dark chocolate, and his hair was unkempt, turning it a dingy blonde. He said nothing more as he closed the door. I let out an exasperated huff. Confusion and fear crawled inside of me. I could feel it everywhere—on my skin, in my guts, closing up my throat, pressing on my temples, and pounding inside my brain. I paced back and forth wildly, gnawing on my lower lip as I did. I wanted to scream, but I knew I shouldn't. So I didn't.

I sat on the edge of my bed and buried my face in my hands. All the questions were stirring and bubbling inside me, and I couldn't make them stop. How did my arm get etched? Why did I have to hide it? Why couldn't I remember anything before Madam and Erin found me? Who had taken Oddy? Was it really all my fault? And the question I didn't want to ask, didn't want to breathe a word of because it was selfish, and because it scared me the most of all, was whether they would come for me next.

I paced and sat and paced some more. Somewhere between those two uncontrollable actions, I fell asleep, crumpled in a ball on top of my bed, exhaustion making that, too, an uncontrollable act.

Seventeen

I awoke not knowing the time of day, but darkness had crept into my room and shadowed over everything. My door had been left open a crack, inviting me to mosey through it. With my throw blanket in tow, I left my room and traveled downstairs. Nothing seemed right. The kitchen echoed with emptiness, and the coffee pot was turned off, even though it was half full.

I strolled out of the kitchen and walked toward dining room. There they all sat—Madam, Erin, Bobby, and Gina. When I entered the room, a small, melancholy chuckle drifted through their semicircle at the opposite end of the table. Their eyes looked bleary, their shoulders sagged, and their coffee mugs were practically empty. Gina's face was sad and heartbroken, and she wasn't chuckling. She was staring off into the distance, her mind in another location.

"Aww, party's over, and crow goes the rooster." Bobby giggled lethargically.

"Morning already?" I asked.

"Oh, man," Erin said, grimacing at the old grandfather clock just outside the dining room. "We gotta go."

"Oh, no," Madam said, running her fingers through her mussed-up hair and staring at the clock as well. "Is it really that early?"

I looked behind me. The clock read 5:37.

"Come on, Basil. We got to get going," Erin said, getting up off his chair and throwing his arms into his jacket. "Get changed and meet me in the shed in ten minutes, all righty?"

I shook my head and turned for the door.

"Wait," Gina said softly.

I spun slowly back around. She was staring straight at me, her large brown eyes full of sorrow.

"Basil, I'm…" She gulped hard. Her eyes turned glassy, and she shook her head back and forth, unable to say anything else.

Everyone gaped at me, as if I were an Interweb flick. I remained silent, gulping as my heart pounded in my ears. A few minutes of awkward silence passed before Erin sprang to life and tugged me out.

*

After changing into a pair of jeans, a gray thermal, and a black sweater, I half-hopped and half-jogged into the shed, feeling the chill of the season on the dirt ground. As I entered the shed, Erin was loading empty barrels onto the carts. It was so cold that our breaths puffed out in dense condensation clouds.

"Here, Basil," Erin said, throwing a black cotton scarf at me. "It's getting kinda cold out. You'll want shoes, too."

I glanced down at my bare feet as a small frown crept across my face. I sulked for a couple of seconds, and then remembered my cold trek to the shed. I started to hunt for the pair of sneakers I kept stored there. After spending too many minutes of my life searching, I found them under our extra units of cables. I shook off the soil and dust that had crusted the rubber, a side effect from stashing them away since the last season, and slipped my feet inside. My toes felt claustrophobic, too confined as I tied the laces.

Grabbing the plastic tubing that attached to the spout at the bottom of the tarps to drain the rainwater, I threw it into one of the carts. I fidgeted with my sneakers, pushing the tips of my soles into one of the rubber wheel. Then I bit my lip and looked over at Erin.

"Is Gina going to be okay?"

Erin focused his eyes on mine, tilting his head slightly as he did, then cleared his throat. "I'm sure she'll be right as rain soon."

For the first time in my life, I didn't believe the certainty in Erin's voice. I clasped my hands together and frowned at the cement.

"What did I do?" I swished my foot against the cement ground, staring at the dirt my shoe moved.

"Huh? What do you mean?" He plopped more empty barrels into the carts.

"Gina said it was my fault. Why?" I asked, pulling over one of the empty barrels.

Erin knelt down in front of me, grasping my shoulders with his giant hands. His face was a mask of seriousness. "Basil, what happened to Oddy has nothing to do with you. Now let's head out." He patted my cheek as he got to his feet.

I took a deep breath, trying to push back my doubt. Erin exited the shed, lugging one of the carts. I hustled after him, hauling the other cart of barrels, and we hiked out to the catching field to empty the fresh rainwater. Erin moved sluggishly, making me wonder if he'd gotten any sleep last night. I got my answer when lunch rolled around. He quickly fell asleep with his arms sprawled out in the grass and his food resting by his head.

My small bowl of gruel sat next to my crossed legs as I mechanically picked at the rind of my beautiful, bright orange. Normally, I would've been delighted to have such a treat for lunch, but my mind wandered. I slipped a slice of orange into my mouth, and as I bit down, the sour citrus juice flooded my mouth. I dropped back, pressing my spine into the ground. My light brown locks mingled with the blades of grass. I tried to stay focused on this—the cool of the grass, the tartness running across my taste buds, the sun playing peekaboo behind the gray clouds, and the solace lingering in the air. I took a deep breath, breathing in the rich, earthy musk of the chilly forest air and smelled rain lingering in the distance.

As I turned onto my side, I felt something skim across my collarbone and tap my shoulder, making my heart skip a beat. I quickly reached inside my sweater and yanked out the thing that had made me jump. Resting on my palm was a small translucent crystal. My breath caught in my throat, and I quickly closed my hand. I clenched my fist, pressing the droplet-shaped gem deeper into my skin.

I took a few preparatory breaths before opening up my hand again. Light bounced off the jewel as if it were winking at me. The tiny crystal reminded me so much of Oddy, and thinking of her made my chest feel tight. I glanced over at Erin, whose soft snores drifted toward me, and then turned my attention back to the crystal. I did that several times, thinking about what had happened the day before, about what had happened to me weeks ago with my etching, and knowing answers were something I wasn't going to get from Erin. As I rose to my feet, I thrust the gem back into my sweater. I took one more glance at him and then ran for the forest.

I felt this sense of boldness swell inside my muscles as I sprinted through the woods toward the manor. I hoped it would stay with me when I approached Gina and asked for the answers everyone wanted to hide from me. I raced up the cobblestone path, and as I passed the shed, something from the corner of my eye made me stop dead in my tracks.

Through the old cracked window of the shed, I saw the back of a man with broad shoulders. It didn't look like Bobby. I dropped to the ground, pressing my back into the wood of the shed as my my heart vibrated against my eardrums. I wrapped my black scarf around my nose and mouth and flipped up my hood, trying to hide the fact that I was a girl—a girl that had been etched years ago. A girl with only questions in her mind. A girl who was quite possibly being hunted. Before I had hashed out a plan, the shed doorknob rasped as it twisted, and the hinges whined as it opened. I leapt for the door and slammed it shut.

"Whoa!" the man said.

"What are you doing here?" I shouted. My voice didn't sound like me. It was laced with bravado I didn't know I possessed.

"Getting water, and it would be a lot easier if I didn't get a door slammed in my face." His voice was lighthearted and nonthreatening.

My boldness was being slowly leeched from my body by fear. I didn't trust this stranger; for all I knew this could be a trick.

"What do you want?" I demanded.

"Water?" he replied, sounding bemused.

The hinges whined, and I threw my shoulder into the door, slamming it shut again. I bit my lip and wedged my foot against the door. It was quiet for a couple of seconds, and then I heard a light knock on the wood.

"Who is this?" he asked.

"Who are you?"

"I asked you first, plus you're the one keeping me hostage." His voice was calm and collected.

"Hostage? You're the intruder!"

"Intruder?" He coughed out a laugh. "I've been called many things, but never an intruder."

The door moved. I pushed against it, but he was stronger, making my shoes skid against the dirt. When the opening was wide enough, he slipped out and let the door fall from his hands. With my added weight, the door banged back into the doorframe. I turned swiftly to face him and slid my back against the wood of the shed, passing the rusted hinges and stepping off the worn dirt path until I was a few feet away from him.

He stood roughly half a foot taller than me and wore khaki pants with lots of pockets, a worn white t-shirt, and scuffed black boots. A paper dust mask covered his nose and mouth, and rubber gloves hung out of his left pocket. A gray sweater was tied around his waist.

"Given?" a woman said, grunting out of the shed, toting a bucket of water. Her copper hair was pulled into a ponytail.

I pushed my back further into the wall of the shed, feeling outnumbered, wishing I could somehow melt right into the wood for safety.

"What happ—" The rest of the woman's sentence drifted into nothingness as she spotted me.

My heart raced as my breaths picked up to match its pace. "You came to steal our water?" Madam had told me stories of robbers coming to stealing their water, back when her family had first started catching. They were stories of warning, of those from the outside.

"What?" The woman's eyes held a puzzled expression. "Are you okay?"

I took a deep breath and shot from the wall, running as fast as I could.

"Wait!" the man called after me.

I kept sprinting, not daring to peek behind me, but a hand grabbed my elbow, pulling me to a stop.

"I think there's been a misunderstanding," the man said, tightening his grip.

I yanked my arm out of his hold and stumbled sideways into the trunk of a tree. I turned to face him, making the tree a safeguard for my back, and eyed him warily. He stepped closer with his palms facing me, open and calm. I couldn't speak; words evaporated off my tongue every time I opened my mouth. That was when I saw the silver glinting from his eyes. I took a step closer to him; fragments of truth lying in his silver eyes pulled me unwillingly toward him. I reached out and gripped his paper dust mask with my fingertips. He didn't flinch or back away from me. He stood still and unmoving as he let me pull his mask from his nose and mouth. He seemed to grow younger, looking closer to my age in a matter of seconds. My fingers dropped from the mask, leaving it to hang around his neck, and I stared at the face of the silver-eyed boy from the forest, the one I was told didn't exist.

"Who are you?" His eyes narrowed curiously at me.

I couldn't speak; all I could do was stare up at him, dumbfounded, feeling like I'd been punched in the chest.

"Given?" The woman with copper hair said, inching toward us.

"It's okay, Mom," the boy—Given—said to her, holding up his hand, signaling her stop.

My eyes jumped back and forth between the two of them. The woman, who looked roughly Bobby's age, didn't resemble Given at all. She had pale skin caked with freckles; her hair was a bright copper; and her eyes were dark brown. The only similarities were their lean build and height, which was intimidatingly taller than I was.

His hand drifted slowly to the side of my forehead. With a gentle finger, he skimmed across my newly formed scar. Understanding illuminated his eyes, and he pulled down my hood and scarf.

His lips cracked into a smile. "It's you."

We stood staring at each other. I partially wondered if my face wore the same expression as his—utter disbelief.

"Basil!" Erin and Madam both shouted at me; Erin was walking toward the manor, and Madam was marching away from it.

Both Given and I flinched at their outburst. Given took a step back, releasing my scarf from his gentle fingers and my eyes from his mesmeric stare.

Erin spat out half-questions as he approached us. "Basil, what happ—how could—why did—"

The woman arrived at our sides at the same time Madam did. All three adults stared at me with bewilderment painted across their faces. My boldness was completely drained, even my reserves, making me want to shrivel into the ground for safety. I gnawed on my lower lip, feeling their stares sink into my skin.

Given was the first to speak; he was eyeing Madam. "You told me she was gone."

"Well…" Madam trailed off, apparently unsure of what to say.

"Why did you lie to me?" he asked. "Because by the way she was talking, it sounds like she lives here."

"When Given brought her in from the woods," the woman with copper hair started, "and I asked you if she was that little girl—"

"Enough!" Erin bellowed. "We don't have to answer any of your questions. Don't you have a job to do, Janie?"

"She is, isn't she?" the woman—Janie—said, taking a step closer to Erin.

"Come on," Erin said, grabbing my arm and pulling me with him.

Given and Janie followed. "Wait!" they both shouted.

"What has gotten into you?" Erin hissed into my ear.

I knew by the way he asked the question that it was rhetorical, but something inside of me cracked, and I couldn't push aside my feelings anymore.

I yanked my arm from his grip. "Because you keep lying to me. Because you won't tell me anything!"

"Basil," he said, sounding shocked.

"Yes, it's partly my fault for letting you, but it's partly your fault for doing it." I could feel all my anger and confusion pressing on my chest. My cheeks felt hot, and my heart began to race. "I was just scared. I'm still scared, but I can't keep living like this. Something feels wrong. I can feel it inside my stomach, eating away at me. I don't want to live like this anymore." I was huffing by the time I finished what I had to say, taking small gasps of air while my heart struggled to slow down.

They all stared at me as if a small tree were growing out of my nose.

"We don't have time for this at the moment," Madam said, coming to life while everyone else remained frozen. "Janie, Given, stay for dinner. We'll converse then." With that, she turned and stalked toward the manor.

Eighteen

I positioned myself at the beige threshold of the manor, pacing back and forth, peering into the forbidden wing. I was supposed to be waiting in my bedroom until someone came to get me for dinner, but I couldn't wait for the hours to pass. I needed answers, and I needed them now. I took a gulp and marched right up to the first door behind the threshold—the room I'd been taken to after hitting my head.

I turned the knob and pushed it open. The room looked the same as it had the last time I'd seen it—velvet blue comforter, white pillows, and a white throw blanket with blue floral sticking. I slinked inside and scanned the plain white walls, then dropped to the ground and searched underneath the bed. Nothing. The next room looked the same, only with a lavender comforter.

The next couple of doors looked exactly like that, but all in different colors. The next door led to a room that actually seemed like it had been lived in—clothes on the floor, paintings hanging on the wall, a lamp sitting on a nightstand, and a bed with a brown comforter. The room looked forgotten; everything sat with an inch of dust covering it. Giant paintings of redwood and oak trees lined the walls of the room, hanging in decorative picture frames.

I shuffled over to the small tea-shaded nightstand and pulled on the worn handle. Inside the little drawer was a small, broken picture frame. Under the shattered glass and layer of dust were two figures. As I brushed off the photo, I recognized one of the figures. A young Bobby stared back at me with his tongue sticking out. His arms were wrapped around a beautiful young woman with a bright, beaming smile. The woman had olive skin, long black hair, and dark brown eyes, exactly like Bobby's description of Lindy. It was then that I realized I was in Bobby and Lindy's room.

I looked at the room with new understanding. The brown comforter reminded me of Bobby's story about their ratty, dirt-colored blanket and how Lindy wouldn't go anywhere without it because it was the first thing they'd bought as a married couple. The paintings on the wall reminded me of the times Bobby had tried to describe Lindy's beautiful artwork, and how she'd loved it when they'd first moved into the manor because it was in the middle of the forest. I remembered how, every time he was away from the kitchen, Bobby always looked sad, like something had been stolen from his heart. Then I saw the room for what it was: a museum of ancient Lindy history. I placed the picture frame back in its drawer and tiptoed out of the room, saying a silent goodbye, just like Bobby said goodbye to Lindy every time he left the kitchen.

I crossed to the next door on the opposite side of the hallway and peeked inside. The room looked like it, too, had been forgotten. It looked like it belonged to a little boy. The walls were painted a light blue, the bed had a blue-and-green striped blanket, and there were clothes spewing out from the armoire. Inching inside, my foot crunched a wrinkled piece of paper. It was tea-colored and the print was faded. The word Missing was printed in big and bold letters on the top of the sheet. There was a physical description of a nine-year-old girl named Rowena. I rummaged around for more papers but found none, so I started searching through the armoire and the little nightstand that had stars painted all over it. Still nothing. Then I crouched down on my hands and knees and searched under the bed. Pushed up against the wall was a small wooden box. I crawled under the bed and pulled it out. A cloud of dust surrounded me, making me sneeze.

The box begged to be opened, and though I knew it was wrong, I did it anyway. It was filled with papers of missing people—not just people, but kids. I pulled out the stack and fanned them across the floor. Underneath the pile was a worn notebook with a leather spine. I flipped it open to a random page toward the middle.

Alex was taken last night. Dad and I went over for our regular card game marathon, but when we showed up, Alex's family was packing to leave. Dad asked them what was going on. Alex's mother kept repeating, "They took him," over and over again. Alex's father said Tabitha and Hanna had been etched, so they were leaving and told my Dad if he were smart, he would do the same. They took him. "They took him." All I hear now in my head is Alex's mother saying, "They took him. They took Alex!"

They etched me two weeks ago. I'm scared. I wish I didn't know. I wish I couldn't see this coming. Maybe I should warn my Dad.

I closed the notebook, feeling my heart shudder. Sitting on the bottom of the wooden box was a photo of Madam and Erin. Between the two of them was a little boy with light brown hair and bright green eyes. I picked up the photo and ran my fingers over all their faces, all smiling carelessly. I'd never seen Madam and Erin look so happy before. For a few painful seconds, my throat closed up with emotion. Madam was watching the little boy from the corner of her eye, as if the picture was taken unexpectedly.

"He was fifteen when—" Erin's voice crept into my ear as it broke painfully. "When he was taken."

"You had a son?" I asked.

My head flinched up, and he was standing at the doorframe, looking into the room with glassy eyes.

"We have a son," Erin said mournfully. "His name—" Erin cleared his throat as his lower lip quivered. "His name is Simon."

"When did it happen?"

"Two years before we found you." He took a seat on the floor while still anchoring himself to the doorframe. "Things were different before. There were lots of kids and families. The outpost had a steady stream of people. The territory wasn't so...so quiet. Yes, things were different, but then..." Erin drifted off, rubbing his face with his hands.

"They were etched," I whispered.

"Eventually all of them. The kids that did speak up told the same story; they said that men in pinstriped suits approached them. These men came out of nowhere, and nobody knew why. The families that tried to run or didn't cooperate were taken and never heard from again. I think that's why Simon never told Maggie or me about his etching."

"He kept it from you?"

"Yeah, he wore that stupid little sweatband." Erin coughed out a tearful laugh as he pointed at my dark green sweatband. "We didn't think anything of it. He saw his friends disappear one by one and still said nothing."

"How long after they etch them do they take them?"

"It varies. A day, weeks. The longest I've ever heard of was two or three months."

"Wait. But I've been with you for eight years. How..." My voice trailed off because I didn't know how to end that question.

Erin shrugged, throwing up his hands. "Maybe it was a one-time thing? Maybe it's because no one really knows you're here? Maybe, you're just—" Erin took a breath, trying to find the right words. "—just different? I don't know, Baze."

"But...Oddy?" Tears filled my eyes. "They took her."

Erin took a deep breath and crawled over to me, placing his hands over mine. "I don't know, Basil. Frankly, there is no precedent for you."

Silence filled the room, and tension lingered in the space separating Erin and me.

"That's how we found you," he said, as if he'd already started the conversation in his head. "We were searching for Simon. I still try to...when I'm at the outpost." He touched my cheek and smiled sadly. "You never forget the people you love. I think that's why Bobby has a hard time when he leaves the kitchen. I'm sure you figured it out, going through his room and all."

"You know I went through his room?" Guilt clouded my voice.

"You're systematic that way."

"Does Lindy sleep in another room?" I asked, but deep inside, I knew that was an irrelevant question.

"Oh Basil," Erin said, turning toward me, "Lindy's been dead for years and years."

"Oh," I whispered, but I felt like I'd always kind of known in a way.

"You have no idea what you did for us, Basil. There was no happiness before you came. We were all heartbroken and grief-stricken. I felt barely human, barely alive."

"Why are you telling me all of this now?" I asked as all the information I'd been wondering about flowed freely from Erin's lips.

"We had always planned on telling you. At first, our excuse was that we thought we should wait until you were older, but then years passed and we never did." He scratched his chin thoughtfully. "We thought we were protecting you by not telling you the truth. I thought by not telling you, I could keep you an innocent little girl." He took a hard swallow. "But then I blinked, and you're seventeen and already know too much about pain. He never told me himself, but I've read Simon's journal, and I know how scared he was. I didn't want that for you."

"Erin—" His name drifted from my lips, but I had no real reply. I just shook my head slowly as his words sank to the bottom of my stomach like heavy bricks.

"You brought so much light with you when you came to live with us. We feared for you more than we feared for our own safety. That's why we kept you hidden. That's why we hid your etching. If anything were to happen to you, I just..." Erin shook his head as he pulled me into his arms.

We stayed like that for a while, Erin holding me as tears trickled from my eyes.

Nineteen

It felt as if I were sitting at the dining room table for the first time. Maybe it was because there was actual bread on the table. Maybe it was because there were guests seated across from me. Or maybe because one of the guests was a boy my age, who was staring at me with a bizarre, half-cocked smile pinned to his face. On the other hand, it was probably all of the above.

I felt like an introvert as I pulled on the long sleeves of my shirt, wadding the fabric up in my palms. Given sat next to Janie in front of me. Bobby was to my right, Madam to my left, and Erin sat at the head of the table. I bit my lip nervously and fiddled with my shirt more.

"We weren't properly introduced. Hi, I'm Janie. Or some people prefer Dr. Hofflin," the copper-haired woman said, giving me a small wave.

"I'm Given," the boy said, with a small, leisurely nod.

"I'm sorry if we scared you, honey," Janie said, taking a bite of bread. "We just didn't know you were here."

"We thought it would be best to have you think she was just passing through," Madam said, patting her napkin against her lips demurely.

"But she's been here all this time, hasn't she?" Janie questioned.

"Yes, she has, and no one has found out about Basil. We would like to keep it that way," Erin said, setting his spoon down inside his bowl of gruel.

"What do you do here?" I asked, ripping off a small piece of bread and nibbling on it.

"We're like a traveling clinic, you could say," Janie said, with a bright, beaming smile.

I must have looked confused, because Given cleared his throat and added, "We go around and help wherever we are needed. Medically speaking, that is."

"Like a health clinic?" I asked, thinking of how Bobby and Erin had talked about large buildings with doctors, medical staff, and equipment.

"Something like that." Janie smiled. "We have actual dates set up for the Manor and a few other places, but mostly we roam around searching for those that need medical attention."

"So you look for disaster?" I asked, one of my eyebrows unintentionally perking up, reminding me of Madam.

Janie and Given looked at each other for a couple of seconds and started to laugh.

"I've never heard it put like that, but I guess we do," said Janie.

"How long have you been doing this?" I asked.

She slowly raised her spoon to her lips and held it there as she thought.

"Ten years or so? I'm not quite sure," she said, finally putting the spoonful of gruel into her mouth.

"Even before I showed up?" I turned to Madam and Erin. "They've been coming here even before then?"

"Well—" Erin looked up, thinking as well. "—just a touch over a year before you showed up."

I looked down into my bowl of gruel, letting the news settle inside my brain. My chest felt tight, and my lower lip felt sore as I began to gnaw on it again. From the corner of my eye, I saw a spoon skid across the table and stopped with a small clink on my bowl. I looked up at Given, who held a slice of bread over his gruel and wore a small, devious smile. When he knew he had my attention, he dipped his bread into the gruel, swirling it around as if it were a gourmet soup. The gruel was too thick, so he ended up having to scoop it onto his bread, and then took a bite. I cringed, and Given laughed. Something about Given's laugh bouncing off the walls made his whole display funny to me, too, and soon we were both laughing.

Twenty

The night passed like calm clouds drifting in the sky, and soon, I was waking up in my bed from the best night's sleep I'd had in a long time. I swam out from under my comforter and pulled my throw blanket around my shoulders. I trotted down the stairs, taunted by the smell of caffeine, and took a seat on my usual stool, breathing in deeply. That was when I realized that it wasn't Bobby's delicious coffee, but his not-so-tasty concoction.

"Morning, Basil," Bobby said, moseying into the kitchen with a handful of handpicked herbs from his garden. "It's crunch time." He placed his fingers between his teeth as if he were nervous.

"You can do it, Bobby." I smiled, scooting closer to him in my stool.

I heard the rasp of wood outside the door and perked up to greet Erin, but I was caught by surprise when Given pushed through the swing door. I had forgotten that Erin had let them stay for the night. Given's steps were sluggish and clumsy as he proceeded to take a seat on the stool farthest from me. He made a pillow for his face by crossing his arms on top of the bar table. He reminded me of a cat curling up for a nap.

Bobby placed a mug of his coffee concoction in front of me, and I stared at the caramel-colored liquid warily.

"You want any, Given?" Bobby asked.

When he didn't respond, Bobby looked at me and shrugged. I took a breath and plopped onto the stool separating the two of us.

"Hello?" I said, poking at his head like he were a rabid animal. "Morning."

Given said something that sounded like a greeting, but his arms muffled it.

"What?"

"Good morning," Given said, turning his head to face me.

I jerked back at the flash of silver. He closed his eyes, turned back into his arms, grumbling a bit, but then turned back to me.

"You want some, Given?" Bobby asked, watching his melodramatic display.

Given yawned, "Want what?"

"Coffee?"

"Coffee?" Given echoed.

"Do you like coffee?" I asked.

"Well..." He sat up, shoulders drooping. "I actually don't."

"You don't?" I leaned back a bit. Bobby's words popped into my head about how to deal with those types of people: run.

Given ran his hands through his dark brown hair and shot me a cockeyed grin. "I'm kidding. I love coffee."

"Great. We're in business, then. How do you like it?" Bobby asked.

"Black, please."

Bobby got him a cup and set it down in front of his crossed arms. I moved back to my original stool.

"I should warn you, though—" I started.

"Shhh, I'm not alive without a cup of coffee in me," Given said, taking a whiff of the mug.

"But I just wanted to let you know that—"

He pressed his index finger to his lips. "Shhhh. Spray can."

"Spray can?"

"That's what you're making me sound like, because you keep talking. Now, shhh."

"Okay, suit yourself." I pulled my throw blanket closer around my arms, as I watched him take another whiff of the deceptive "coffee."

Given blew on it and took a sip. I waited for his face to squish up from the dirt-like quality of the concoction, but he never did. In fact, he took another long, gulp-like swig. I took a sip of my own to see if I had gotten it wrong, but the dirt taste hit me right after the coffee taste did. Given downed the whole mug in a matter of minutes.

"Taste good?" I asked.

"Mmmhmm," he said, staring at the bottom of his mug longingly.

Bobby was stirring a dry mixture in a large plastic bowl. Given got up and poured himself another mugful. Bobby threw some more flour into the bowl as Given leaned against the cabinets like he was at home.

"Bobby, right?"

"Yeah." Bobby shook Given's proferred hand.

"It's been a while," Given said.

"Five years?" Bobby turned to me. "After they did their whole clinic thing, Given used to hang out with me."

"What happened?" I asked.

"Madam," Given said. "She banished me from ever stepping foot into this kitchen."

"What? Really?"

"No." Given chuckled with a half-cocked smile. "It felt like it, though. It just felt more businesslike. The more time passed, in and out. Now that I think about it, though, she was probably worried about you."

"Yes, I guess," I said, shrugging my shoulders and taking another sip of my coffee. I cringed as the taste hit my tongue. I turned to Given. "You really like this?"

"What's not to like?"

"It's not coffee, though. Real coffee tastes like roasted beans. Real coffee taste." I looked down at my mug and wrinkled my nose. "Good."

Given chuckled and took another swig. "This is the best I've ever had. Besides, after Tafy's coffee, this is like gold."

"Really?" I asked, thinking of the time of the month he usually came, less than a week before the big supply run.

"Oh, yeah. Tafy's coffee will put hair on your chest to say the least."

"Who's Tafy?" I asked.

"A chef further down the territory. He's real hard-nosed, but you gotta love him."

Madam and Janie pushed past the swinging door and perched at the end of the bar table.

"Good morning, Gives," Janie said with a bright smile. She was clearly more of a morning person than Given. "Good morning, hon."

It took me a second to realize she was talking to me.

"Morning," I said timidly, smiling up at her.

"You ready to head out?" Janie asked, hitting Given lightly on his shoulder.

"Yup."

Madam and I followed them out of the manor, where a black SUV waited. Janie turned to me and pulled me into a hug. My limbs stiffened in her embrace.

"It was really nice to meet you again." She pulled away and looked down at me. "I'm glad you are doing well." She smiled once more and went back to Madam.

Given's body language was awkward as his eyes wandered around. He took a breath and rested his silver, alien eyes on me.

"Well, I guess this is goodbye," I said, unable to fight the bashfulness that fell over my words.

Given cocked a half-smile, gazing at me as he tilted his head. "Goodbye? No. Listen to me, Basil; this is anything but goodbye."

"See you later?" I posed.

He smiled. "See you soon."

We stood there awkwardly in front of one another, unsure of how we should end it. As he titled his face up, the sunlight caught his eyes and made them flicker an intense silver. The overwhelming feeling of familiarity swelled inside my stomach.

"Given?" I asked before I even realized his name was on my lips.

"Yes?" He bent his knees, lowering slightly to meet my eyes.

Something about that gesture was intimidating, as if I could hide in the space that separated my height and his. But now that buffer was gone, and I felt extremely shy and nervous having him stare at me straight on. I fidgeted with my throw blanket timidly.

"What is it?" he asked.

"Have we ever met before?"

"Yes."

I bit my lip and glanced over at Madam and Erin, who were busy saying their farewells to Janie. I turned back to Given. "When?"

"A month ago. I was getting water when I heard something strange in the woods. I went to investigate and found you. I took you back to the Manor—fixed your arm, stitched you up. You don't remember any of it, do you?" His eyes were narrowed, inquisitive.

"I do. Well, bits and pieces of it, actually, but what I meant was, have we ever met b—"

"Well, we'd better hit the road, Given," Janie said, patting him on the back.

"Come on, Basil, we have a lot of rain catchers to empty," Erin said, waving me over.

Given hopped into the passenger's seat, and Janie sat behind the wheel. The SUV's engine rumbled to life and started to roll away. I rushed up to Given's window and knocked on the glass frantically. He rolled it down as curiosity washed over his face.

"Have we ever met before, then?" I asked in a rush, not knowing why I had to know so badly.

Given's eyes narrowed. "Why do you ask?"

I wanted to tell him the feelings I'd been having, like I knew him from somewhere, and I couldn't quite put my finger on where. Janie leaned over, waving at me to say goodbye as Erin clutched my arm and waved back. I could tell Given wanted to say something, but with all the commotion, Janie ended up driving away before he could.

Twenty-One

I wrapped my black scarf around my nose and mouth, trying to trap my body heat inside. As the weeks passed, the weather had finally peaked, and everything was coated in a dense layer of frost. I tucked my scarf into my sweater and flipped up my hood.

"You got it, Baze?" Erin asked, looking up at the wooden pole that had a broken ring at the top.

"Yeah," I said, rubbing my temple, trying to quell the headache that seemed to be as persistent as the cold.

Erin and I had recently emptied all the rain catchers. Now we were able to buy out time to fix the ones that had taken a beating from the storms. I blew into my hands, filling them with warmth. Erin handed me an extra metal ring. I tucked it into my sweater pocket and climbed up the wooden pole. At the top, I planted my feet on the small platform and pulled off the broken ring, slipping it into the pocket of my jeans. I reached out and grabbed the corner of the tarp that fluttered freely in the wind, clipped the ring onto it, and then attached it to the top of the pole.

"Okay, all set," I said as I climbed down. "Here you go." I handed Erin the broken ring, hoping it was in good enough shape to repair.

"Hey, you," a voice called from behind.

I turned around and was surprised to see Given standing a few yards away, staring at me with those silver, extraterrestrial eyes. It felt like so much time had passed since I'd last seen him. Enough time had passed that Gina had finally been able to head back to her house; Bobby had finished his orders and started on a new set; and Erin had made his monthly trip to the outpost to pick up new supplies. Everything had moved in such order that it almost felt like the whole unveiling of Given's existence had never happened. But here he was, standing before me, or as much as I could see of him past all the dirt.

"Hey, kid!" Erin shouted.

Given smiled. "Hey, Erin."

"Hi." I smiled, hesitating a moment or two before approaching him.

Given's long-sleeved thermal and khaki pants were caked with dirt. His face was speckled with mud, and his right ear was completely covered in something thick and black.

"What happened?" I asked, pointing at his ear.

"Oh, that's right, you've never seen me pre-manor before," he said, with a small chuckle. "Side effect of the job. What's your excuse?" He pulled my scarf away from my face and looked down at my dirt-covered shoes and jeans.

I grinned shyly. "Same."

"Well," Erin said, squinting up at the sun, which had been playing peekaboo with us all day. "It's 'bout time to head in."

We started our trek back to the manor, shoes crunching on frozen leaves and grass.

"So—you're early," Erin said.

"Yeah, a day early. Well, with the secret all out in the open, we were hoping you wouldn't care. You guys are my favorite stop."

"Geesh, kid, any more butter, and I'm gonna need some bread to swallow it all." Erin laughed. "Besides, you only like us for our washrooms."

Given threw his hands up into the air like he was surrendering. "I'm caught. I feel so ashamed." He wore a half-cocked smile that suggested otherwise.

We headed up the cobblestone path that led to the back of the manor. We stomped into the small mudroom and peeled off layers of dirt-covered clothes, shedding sneakers and rolling up mud-soaked jeans. Given and Erin did the same. As we entered the kitchen, three buckets of water sat on the countertop, awaiting our arrival.

Erin chuckled. "See, this is all you love about us."

"No," Given said, dipping his fingers into the water, "but it's a perk."

Madam peeked her head in, holding the swinging door open. "Basil, library in fifteen minutes."

"Okay," I said, pulling one of the buckets off the counter.

Given followed Erin out the swinging door, and I trekked up the stairs through the pantry. After I was all cleaned up, I headed down to the library for my study session with Madam. As I stepped inside the warm-colored library, I saw a familiar novel resting on the desk. I knew exactly what that meant.

"I need you to read to Madeline tonight," Madam said, sorting through a stack of papers. "I have a lot of catching up to do, and I'm sure she would love your company."

I bit my lip nervously and ran my fingers across the imprinted title on the cover of the novel, The Fair Maiden's Tale, which I'd read to her countless times before. It was her favorite.

"Okay," I said hesitantly.

"I'll go with Basil," Given's voice shot out from the doorframe of the library.

"Great. She's expecting you, Basil," Madam said, strutting out of the room.

I picked up the book and headed out the door to the giant staircase. Madeline was a wily woman who hated being stuck in bed. Part of me felt like she didn't like me because I didn't get her humor very well. Given followed me through the hallway and up to her bedroom. I knocked lightly on the door and stepped inside.

"Hello, Madeline." I smiled tiptoeing up to her bed.

Madeline turned over, her mattress squeaking, and adjusted her shirt with her frail fingers. She pushed her short, gray hair away from her face as she blinked up at us with drained, green eyes.

"Hello, child," Madeline said with a small smile, but when she looked over at Given, the smile dissipated. "Oh, bother. Look what the cat dragged in. Given, my boy, you're looking mischievous as always."

My mouth dropped open as I stared at Madeline's narrowed eyes. A small spark ignited the green around her pupils.

"And look at you, you old coot. Up to no good as always?" Given coughed back at her as a laugh tumbled from his lips.

"With these old bones, I can only get away with ruining your day."

"Well, then, I guess it's a good thing I drew the short straw today and they're forcing me to check up on you."

"They're just waiting for me to keel over and croak," Madeline told me.

"Oh, you're too feisty of a gal for that to happen anytime soon," Given said, waving her statement off with his hand.

"I know you're the leader planning the party."

"I prefer chairman, actually, and who told you?"

She pressed a delicate hand to her chest. "I still have my ways."

My eyes grew wide as saucers as I glanced back and forth between the two of them, seeing their faces painted with sarcasm.

"She's a skittish little thing, isn't she?" Madeline said, pointing at me.

"I know, but you've got to admire her attempt," Given said, patting me on my arm. "Then again, you know what they say," he said with a shrug of his shoulders. "It's the quiet ones you gotta look out for."

"In-ter-es-ting," Madeline said, pronouncing every syllable slowly, and leaned in closer to me.

I gave a small, weary smile, clutching the novel as if it could shield me somehow.

"I see it," Madeline said, poking her finger in my direction. "You're planning something, aren't you?"

"Ummm," I said, unsure of how to respond.

"Just say yes," Given whispered into my ear.

"Yes?" I said, making it sound more like a question than an actual reply.

"I knew it," Madeline said, tapping her forehead with her index finger. "I can see your intelligent mind ticking behind those big green eyes of yours. You fool me not, child."

Given grabbed my arms and spun me around, forcing me to stare into his vibrant gaze. He glanced back over at Madeline. "With those big, beautiful eyes of hers, she could be planning something really devious."

My cheeks sizzled as I turned back around to face Madeline. I bit my lip and tugged on my hair. "So you two know each other?"

Madeline chuckled. "Unfortunately."

"We go way back," Given said. "I've had to put up with her for a long time."

"You put up with me? Please, I'm a dream."

"Nightmare's more like it."

"You're the monster that lurks under children's beds." Madeline giggled. "I don't know how you managed to snag the eye of this fair maiden here."

My cheeks flushed an even deeper shade of crimson, as I began to feel even more nervous and embarrassed.

"We're not—" I whispered, shaking my head vigorously back and forth.

"Well, this fair maiden happens to put up with me quite nicely."

"I don't know how she does it," Madeline replied with a dramatic frown.

"Speaking of fair maidens," I said, clearing my throat, "why don't I start reading?"

"Oh, no. We'd better settle down now. I think we're embarrassing Basil here," Given said, pulling over one of the armchairs.

"We? You are," Madeline said.

"Oh, all right. I'll let you win this one," he said with a surrendered bow to Madeline. He turned to me then. "I'm a total embarrassment, and I'm deeply sorry. Can you ever forgive me, Basil?"

His eyes were wide and endearing, and his hands lay open and apologetic. I looked over at Madeline, who was shaking her head, throwing her fist into her palm. I don't know what came over me. Maybe it was the way Given tilted his head sweetly, or the way Madeline's smile was lined with pluckiness, but I blurted out, "Dear Sir, you are not forgiven," as if I were the fair maiden from Madeline's favorite novel.

One corner of Given's lips shot straight up toward the ceiling. Madeline laughed so hard she started to cough.

"But I brought you treasures and the like," Given said, acting as the offended gentleman of the novel.

"Treasures are no way to a woman's heart." I pressed my hand to his chest and threw my head in the opposite direction theatrically.

"Your reputation says otherwise."

"Then someone has filled your mind with lies."

Given looked away for a second, and I almost thought he had forgotten his next line, but then he turned back to me with a mischievous grin. "I must confess that the gifts were a test."

"A test? Why, sir, what a devious thing to do. You may take your leave."

Given took the novel from my hands and placed it on Madeline's small nightstand near her bed. He knelt down on one knee and grabbed my hand. "Will one forgive if the apology is true and heartfelt?"

"If one is true and heartfelt, I will consider, but you, sir, are neither,." I ripped my hand out of his.

Madeline sat up straighter, clasping her hands together in an endearing kind of way. Her lips burst into a smile, and her eyes turned glassy.

"You do not remember, do you?" Given got to his feet slowly. "You do not remember me at all. I brought you forget-me-nots just so you wouldn't forget."

"Forget-me-nots!" I shouted, because this was the big, dramatic climax of the novel.

"Yes, I brought them just for you, my fair maiden. And after you accepted them, accepted me, we would dance all night long," he said as he grabbed my hands and whirled me around the room.

Madeline clapped her hands rhythmically, giving us a beat to keep tempo. Given twirled me up and down and around the bedroom as if it were a magnificent ballroom. Madeline giggled like a child watching a wondrous play that enveloped her inside her favorite fantasy.

"I do remember!" I shouted.

Given took that as a cue to slow down his pace. He spun me slowly and dipped me right in front of Madeline, who clapped as we took a bow.

"And they lived happily ever after. The end," said Given.

"Oh, I just love that story. Basil, you were wonderful. Given, you were...meh," she said, shrugging her shoulders.

The three of us erupted into a chorus of laughter. Madeline's laugh turned into a hacking cough. Given sat next to her and rubbed her arm until she settled down.

"Well, young lady, I think we should let you get some sleep," he said, getting to his feet.

"Yeah, let the old coot get some rest in peace," Madeline said, but sadness flickered in her eyes.

I clutched the novel and whispered, "Sleep well, Madeline."

"We'll be back another time." Given smiled, slowly closing her door. "Promise."

The hallway had darkened; the sun's light was a shade of dark pink as it peeked in through the few windows along the walkway. Our bare feet made the floorboards creak.

"So you know the story?"

"I must have read it to her a million times by now," I said, thinking of the days when I'd first started to read to her. My feet had dangled from the armchair, unable to touch the floor. I stole a glance at Given; the light made his face softer and his hair darker. "So how do you know the story so well?"

"One of the families we visited one territory over gave us the book as a thank you. It was the first book that didn't have the words 'cauterize' or 'hemorrhage' as one of its chapters. Let's just say I was grateful for the variety."

Laughter lingered between us for a few carefree seconds.

"Do you like the story?"

"What's not to like?" Given shrugged and looked over at me. "Wait, you don't?"

I shrugged, clasping my hands together. "Why can't they just say what they mean?"

It was silent for a while. Our footsteps sounded louder in the quiet hallway. I kept my focus straight ahead, zeroing in on the first step of the giant staircase.

"Your eyes carry the soft spring meadow and shine, as if the pasture were sprinkled with crystals."

His voice drifted to my ears softly, making my heart sputtered in my chest—an awkward rhythm that was clumsy and filled my face with heat. I was suddenly grateful that the hallway was splashed with a hue of pink. I hadn't realized that Given had stopped moving until I turned to face him; he was several feet behind me.

An awkward smile pulled at his lips. "I mean, doesn't that sound better than, 'Your eyes are a pretty green color?'" His voice was an unsure whisper.

"I… I guess," I stuttered nervously, clutching the novel close to my chest.

He ran a hand through his hair and shrugged uncomfortably, making me wonder what he was thinking of. Given cleared his throat, but didn't say anything. We started to travel down the hallway again. A light set of footsteps came from the stairs, and soon, Madam came into view.

"Basil, Given, I was just about to get you two. Bobby needs some help with dinner."

"Okay," Given and I said in unison, thankful for the break in the awkward silence.

Twenty-Two

I was in the kitchen, stirring a pot of gruel and thinking about Madeline, how I'd never seen her act so freely with me, not to mention her calling my mind intelligent. I looked over at the stool where I had placed The Fair Maiden's Tale, and it made me think of the first time I'd ever been told to read to Madeline. I padded into her room, practically shaking. I hadn't told Madam or Erin that she scared me, probably because I wasn't sure why or when that fear started. I sat in Madeline's room with the novel between us, and she spouted off a few quick, sarcastic sentences, which pulled me out of my comfort zone and turned me mute with tears. Ever since then, she'd never really talked to me.

"Will the lovely fair maiden be so kind as to tell me what is on her mind?" Given asked.

"Huh?" I looked up to see Given staring at me as he mixed a bowl of dry ingredients. I glanced over at Bobby, who was kneeing a mountain of dough.

"You look lost in thought."

"You'll get used to it," Bobby shouted to Given.

Given's eyes narrowed, intrigue on his face.

"Oh, I was just thinking about Madeline," I said, directing my attention to the pot of gruel.

"Fiery, isn't she?"

"Yes. Yes, she is," I said, staring intensely at the brown, grainy goop at the end of my wooden spoon.

"You certainly made her day."

"Me?" I looked up at Given, perplexed. "Oh, no, that was all you."

He smiled into his bowl. "Well, I haven't seen her that lively in a while."

I stared at Madeline's favorite novel resting on the stool and wondered why that was so.

"There it is again."

"What?"

"That haze of pensiveness," Given said, brushing his hand past my face for emphasis.

"I guess I just mull over my memories a lot," I said, now stabbing the gruel with my spoon.

"Hmm. Why is that?"

I shrugged mechanically but curled my shoulders forward, almost wishing I could hide from his probing stare.

"Are you afraid of losing them?"

I dropped my spoon into the pot, and my heart stuttered. His question hit close to home; it scared me. I didn't like that he seemed to be figuring me out quicker than I could figure him out. Or maybe he was giving me a clue. Maybe he was drawing from experience. I stared at my green sweatband and then glanced at Given's arms. His long-sleeved white thermal covered them both.

I picked up the spoon and resumed my stirring. "Why do you ask?"

"Just throwing out theories here," Given said, setting down the bowl. "Just let me know when I'm getting warm."

I could see Bobby eyeing me from afar, making me feel like my forearm wasn't covered enough. Both of their stares made me wish I had opted to wear one of my long-sleeved shirts instead of my ratty gray tee with a picture of an ancient band logo that involved an animated skyline of skyscrapers.

Janie and Madam both walked into the kitchen mid-conversation. Madam was nodding her head as Janie proceeded with her story. I was grateful for their interruption.

"He looked so adorably stubborn." Janie chuckled. "His eyes all determined."

"Oh, no. Not that story again," Given said, picking up his bowl and stirring with newfound vigor.

"Oh, come on, Given. It's such a cute story," Janie said.

Given turned his focus to the dry mixture that really didn't need any more attention.

"So, of course, I told Given absolutely no." Janie shot another smirk at Given. "Well, the next day, we were way down in one of the lower territories; they had just been hit with a major storm, and trees and debris were everywhere. I told Given to stay in the car, like always, and then ran out to help. Not fifteen minutes passed before I saw Given helping this man who'd had a tree crash into his house. He calmed him down and bandaged him up like a pro. When things quieted down, I went up to Given, full of anger and fury, but he gazed up at me with those big, innocent eyes and said, 'I just have to Mom.'" Janie placed her hand on her chest. "My heart just burst into pieces right there."

Madam nodded.

"Ever since then, he's been helping me," Janie said with a shrug.

"Wow, he's really somethin'," Bobby said, punching Given playfully on the shoulder.

"Yeah, he is. He has really excelled so quickly. It's rather remarkable." Janie sighed. "I'm so grateful to be given such a great kid."

Dull laughter passed through the group of adults. I looked over at Given, and he was staring into his bowl with a modest stance and coy smile.

"Anyways, how've you been, Bobby?" Janie asked.

"I've been good," Bobby said, breaking up the heap of dough into little patties.

"How did you know what to do?" I whispered to Given as Madam and Janie talked to Bobby about the progress with his monthly orders.

Given was so quiet and focused on his mixing that I almost thought he didn't hear me. He took a small breath and looked over at me.

"Before I started helping my mom, I would just wait in the SUV," he said, letting the dry batter slip off his plastic spatula. "For hours on end. I had a lot of time on my hands, to say the least. A lot of time where I mostly read, and being that my Mom is a doctor, most of the material I could find was medically related."

"You taught yourself?"

"Well?" Given looked up, apparently trying to think back. "It gave me the basics. My mom walked me through the more complicated procedures. I just couldn't…," Given shook his head and set down the bowl. "I couldn't keep sitting in that SUV when I'm very capable of helping someone."

"So you went out and did it."

"Yes." He took a breath. "Well, working in theory with words and paper is very different than working with people made of flesh and bone."

Given pushed up his sleeves and leaned against the counter. His eyes were coated with seriousness. He did a couple of standing pushups, making my eyes lock on his forearms. His skin lay clean and unblemished. There was no pucker of scarred flesh, no sleek, precise mark. His forearm was tanned and perfectly smooth.

"The first time was the hardest and the scariest," he said, standing up straight with his expression the grimmest I'd ever seen it. "It was stupid and dangerous for me to do it so carelessly."

"Why is that?"

"You know, with all the kids turning up missing, having me out on the loose wasn't the best idea." He shook his head. "As you can tell by the story, my mom was completely against it at first."

"So you know about the missing kids? When did you find out?"

Given gave me a dubious look. "I've always known. Why do you ask?"

I bit my lip and glanced at the group of adults. Bobby and Janie threw their heads back with laughter. I turned back to Given with bashful eyes. "I just found out about a month ago."

"Oh." He looked taken aback, seeming caught off guard by my confession.

"Umm…yeah," I said, shifting my eyes from left to right as embarrassment filled my cheeks with heat.

"Well, you know what makes me feel better?" he asked, as if he could see the pain painted around my eyes.

"It's okay…" I trailed off shaking my head and holding up my hand.

The conversation died as I turned to the pot of gruel with a small, sad smile. Silence lingered between us; the only sounds I heard were Janie's snorting laughter and the gruel sticking to the end of my spoon. I turned back around, and a flicker of light caught my eye, drawing my attention to a necklace I hadn't noticed before around Given's neck. It was a tiny, silver, rectangular prism, half an inch long and a couple of centimeters wide. There were three lines running around the end of the rectangle, and it was attached to a silver chain. Like everything else about Given, the necklace looked oddly familiar.

Suddenly, Bobby came up behind me and peeked into the pot of gruel. He leaned in, taking a big whiff, as if it were a mouthwatering stew. "Dinner time."

Twenty-Three

Dinner came and went in a quick, orderly fashion with Janie supplying most of the conversation. After dinner, I had my usual studies and then headed off to bed. I was lying on my bed, fingering through Madeline's favorite novel, wondering why she loved it so much, not to mention Given liking it as well. I'd always viewed the story as something cheesy and cliché in a "love never dies" kind of way. But the way, Madeline got all giddy, and Given got all...Given about it made me think that maybe I'd missed something. I flipped through it more quickly, scanning it as I did, until I reached the end. I flung the back of the book shut, but then something caught my eye. I opened it again, and right behind a small handful of blank pages, written directly onto the back of the cover was:

Eighteen years of servitude and counting. Love you, my Fair Maiden.
Your Hubby,
Hobart

My heart felt as if it were being squeezed tight with emotion. It made me wonder if reading this story for Madeline was like being in the kitchen for Bobby—a breathable piece of who they used to be with their loved ones. On this thought, I got up, wrapped my throw blanket around my arms, and headed out the door. I marched all the way to Madeline's room. I took a deep breath before knocking quietly on her door, then cracked it open and peeked inside. Madeline's figure was barely visible as she lay atop her bed in the dark. I wondered if she were asleep, but then a bright light beamed on me.

"Basil?" Madeline's voice sounded puzzled. "Come in, child."

I shuffled in, gripping the novel as if it were a life preserver in the intimidating sea, and pulled over one of the armchairs next to her bed. She pointed her flashlight at the novel.

"I hope I didn't wake you up," I whispered.

"Oh, dear child, my age makes it hard to sleep," Madeline mused.

Her eyes looked sad and tired, but her lips were pressed into a small, reserved smile. At that very moment, I wondered how I could have ever been afraid of her. I gave a tiny smile in return and held up The Fair Maiden's Tale.

"I was wondering if you would like to be my audience," I said through pursed lips.

"Oh." Madeline's eyes grew wide with bewilderment. "Oh, okay."

I cracked open the novel and started. I read all through the night as though it were the first time. I grew a new appreciation for all the words that were carefully selected and entwined together, trying to see how each artistic expression was from the character's heart. I kept reading long after Madeline drifted off to sleep, and the quietness crept in all around me. I read until I came to Madeline's note from her husband. I left her room just as dawn settled in.

As I headed downstairs with clumsy, lethargic steps, the sensation of overwhelming jubilation filled my lungs. I staggered into the kitchen, intoxicated with triumph and slight delirium from lack of sleep. Instead of sitting at my usual stool, I decided to be daring and get my own cup of coffee. I made it just the way I liked it and took a big, eager gulp. The coffee tasted like victory and then dirt. I quickly swallowed Bobby's coffee concoction. My body jerked with its disgusting descent. I moved to a stool as Bobby tromped in with two buckets of water.

"Morning, Baze," Bobby chimed, setting the buckets on the countertop farthest from me.

"Morning," I said, taking a small sip of my coffee.

The swinging door opened slowly as Given sluggishly emerged through it. He sat down on a stool and laid his head on the bar table, half-asleep. Bobby looked at Given and shook his head as he chuckled.

"Morning!" I cheered, leaning in closer to Given so he could hear.

Given grumbled some kind of inaudible complaint and pulled his arms in closer to his face. Bobby placed a mug of black coffee next to him and went to working on an order that involved buttercream. Given slowly sat up, yawning as he did. His silver eyes were ringed with weariness, and his shoulders stooped forward with tiredness.

"You're not much of a morning person, are you?" I posed, pushing his mug of coffee closer.

Given shook his head as he placed his index finger to his lips. "Shhh. Pretty things shouldn't talk this early in the morning."

He did another deep yawn and ran a hand through his short, dark hair. As he picked up his mug and proceeded to drink it, I contemplated his hair. It was a Mohawkish sort of style, in the fact that the majority of his hair ran down the center of his head. What made it interesting was the preciseness of his cut; there were two horizontal shaved lines over his right ear.

"How did you cut your hair like that?" I asked without thinking.

Given downed his coffee and poured himself another cup before moving to the stool closest to me.

"I just know the right people." He took another gulp of his coffee. "Well, my mom knows the right people."

Bobby and Erin had been sporting the same hairstyle for as long as I could remember, and I only took scissors to my hair when it got too unmanageably long. I pulled at a clump of my hair, examining the tips of my light brown tendrils. It ran well past my shoulders in a limp, lackluster way.

"Azalea," Given said.

"What?" I asked.

"That's the name of the woman who cuts my hair, Azalea. She lives in the middle territories. Territory 76, I think?" Given leaned in as he squinted his eyes almost all the way closed, and mimicking an old woman's voice, he said, "Given, is that you?" He placed his hands atop his own head, patting several times. "Ahh, it is you. Come in, boy. Your hair is much too long. I'm just gonna give ya a trim." He laughed taking another swig of his coffee. "She can hardly see a thing, but she does good work."

I found myself laughing along with him, the jubilation stirring inside my stomach even more. I took another sip of my coffee, wincing at the taste.

"Wait right here," Given said, running out of the kitchen.

I looked at Bobby, who seemed as puzzled as I was.

"Coffee really perks him up," he said, turning back to the cake he was frosting.

Given came back into the kitchen, carrying a notebook and a pen. He sat down and fingered through pages decorated with words, pictures, and odd things like feathers and beads pasted onto the thick, coarse paper. He kept flipping until he came to a clean sheet. I watched his fingers as he drew four lines that intersected one another. He put an X in the center, and then understanding pummeled me – it was tic-tac-toe.

"I was trying to tell you last night," he said. "It's kind of corny."

"What isn't corny about you?" I said with a wily smile.

He looked at me with an impressed half-smile, but I wished I could eat my words.

"Sorry," I muttered, curling my shoulders forward, boldness making me feel awkward.

Given ignored my comment as he proceeded with his original thought. "This is what makes me feel better."

"Tic-tac-toe?"

"Yup," he smiled and handed me the pen.

When I was younger, I would play tic-tac-toe with Bobby and Erin all the time. I distinctly remembered Bobby and Erin discussing whether the Xs and Os were kisses or hugs. Bobby's take was that Xs were hugs because the lines were stretching out to give you a hug, and the Os were kisses because lips make an O shape when you kiss someone. Bobby would then back

147

up his argument by kissing the top of my head, making sure he pointed out the shape his lips made. Erin said that the Os were the hug, because it's round like it's encircling someone. Erin would also back his statement by pulling me into a hug.

"What are you thinking about?" Given asked, lowering his eyes to meet mine.

"Oh, umm, just Xs and Os and what they mean." My face flushed as I thought about Bobby's and Erin's kisses-versus-hugs debate. "It's nothing," I said, putting an O on the top right corner.

"So you've played this before."

"A lot."

I thought back to when I'd first arrived at the manor. I'd been scared and alone. Erin had showed me how to play this game as some sort of peace offering. It was what ultimately inspired me to trust him.

"Me too." Given smiled placed an X under his other one. "Were you thinking about the unresolved dispute on what the Xs and Os stand for?"

"Aaah, yeah," I said softly. My eyebrows rose as my cheeks flushed hotter. I blocked his attempt by putting an O to the left of my original mark. "The whole hugs-versus-kisses thing, right?"

"Yeah. You know what I think?" He put an X on the bottom-left corner.

I remained silent as I put an O on the bottom right, blocking his victory.

"I think the debate is silly," he said, tapping the pen on his lip.

"Why is that?"

"Because you can't have one without the other; you can't have an X without an O," he answered, keeping his eyes trained on the game, trying to figure out where to mark next.

"Yeah, like if it were a mathematical equation, you wouldn't be able to equal them out unless they were together."

Given looked up. "Did you just win?"

I looked down and realized that no matter where he placed his mark, I would win. A smile crept across my face. "I think I did."

"You're distracting me," he said through playfully narrowed eyes as he marked the top left corner.

I put an O in the center of the right column, winning the game. As I set up a new game, I said, "It's just illogical when the Xs and Os are apart."

"No." Given stared intensely at the paper, "it's less rational than that." He looked up at me with a half-cocked smile. "Don't try to rationalize everything."

"What?"

"Tick, tick, tick. That's what you do in that head of yours." His smile widened, and I knew he thought he had figured out at least that aspect about me.

"Well," I said, taking a deep breath, feeling like he knew too much.

"Well, what?" he asked, lifting up one of his eyebrows.

"Well, we all can't be spontaneous medics."

He chuckled. "Spontaneous medics?"

"You're used to going wherever the wind takes you."

"Going wherever the wind takes me? Hmm, how does that relate?"

"Going wherever the wind takes you in life, in thoughts and ideas," I said, pointing at him. "You're carefree that way. You're..." I trailed off, trying to think of a better adjective.

"Irrational that way?" He posed. "So how does the whole medic thing fit in, then?"

"Well, that's just you. You go around helping people. You fix up their outsides while trying to calm their insides. You come to their rescue when tragedy strikes." I grinned, feeling loopy from lack of sleep. "And they're so grateful that they give you haircuts and coffee that puts hair on your chest and books and dirty clothes and—"

"Okay, I'm gonna have to stop you right there," Given interrupted, grabbing the finger that I didn't know I was still pointing at him.

"First of all, what are you drinking? And second, you got it all wrong."

"First of all, I'm drinking coffee, same as you. Secondly, I haven't slept. And thirdly of all—" I paused knowing that didn't sound quite right. "What did I get wrong?"

He hesitated for a moment. "Well, nothing. You just..." He trailed off, squirming with awkwardness. "You just make me sound all heroic."

"Well, aren't you, in a way?"

"You remember everything I've said, don't you?" he asked, an amazed look in his eyes. "Do you forget anything?"

I frowned, and I could tell Given knew he'd hit a nerve.

"Hey," he cooed in a voice I could see him using on someone who was about to slip into shock. "You can tell me, you know."

I leaned away from him, wondering what he knew. "Tell you what?" I kept my voice low for fear Erin or Madam might hear.

150

They'd conditioned me never to speak of my etching or my lost memories, but maybe I had unintentionally given something away. Maybe he knew about my secret, and just maybe I could confide in him.

"What's bothering you so much?" Given's silver eyes had softened with calmness, the way they turned when he was being sincere.

Gnawing on my lower lip, wavering between completely denying it or admitting the truth, I pulled my throw blanket closer to my chest and turned to my cup of coffee. I couldn't tell him my secret. I'd been hiding it too long. I thought maybe even a part of me didn't believe it.

"It's nothing," I said, looking up at him with a small half-smile.

Given lowered his eyes until he was staring straight at me in that intimidating but honest way of his.

"Yeah, right, Basil." He was blunt and straightforward in a nice way only he could get away with.

"It's—" I gulped, knowing I couldn't hide from him. "It's nothing I can't handle."

Madam marched into the kitchen, and Erin trailed quietly behind.

"Basil, you and Erin need to be out of here in forty minutes," Madam said, tucking her hair behind her ear.

"Madam," I said, clearing my throat, trying to build up courage. "I was wondering if I could stay here."

"No."

"Well—" Erin sighed.

Madam gasped. "Erin."

"I don't think it's a bad idea. We don't have much to do anyway. Might as well stay here and be of some kind of help," Erin said, getting a cup of coffee.

Madam was quiet as she thought it through. Finally, she took a sharp breath and said, "Fine, but Basil stays in the kitchen with the door locked."

My face broke into a smile as I took a victorious sip of my coffee.

Twenty-Four

It was like nothing I'd ever experienced. The manor was hustling and bustling with people, which both frightened and excited me. It was as if the manor groaned and sighed all on its own, transforming into a living being that was alive with activity. As I mixed a bowl of cookie dough, I could hear the people through the walls. The soles of their shoes clacked against the hardwood floor. Their coughs echoed through the corridors. The wood creaked when they sat down, and their voices were muffled as they spoke.

Wonder and curiosity filled me; I wanted to see for my own eyes the event that was taking place outside the kitchen. I took the small stepping stool and pushed it up against the swinging door. As I stepped onto the stool, I peeked out the little window that had clouded with age.

It was like peering into another world, a world with aliens that walked, talked, and looked like me. They were all older than I was, of course, but their faces were all the same – sad and downhearted. Janie and Given slowly made their way from one patient to the next, both wearing paper masks and rubber gloves. Given wore a gray sweatshirt with the hood flipped up, aging his appearance. I wondered if that was how he got away with no one taking a second glance at him.

I could see so much of Janie in him, the way his eyes lit up softly when he talked with a patient, and how he gripped a few of their hands in a reassuring way. They nodded their heads in the same manner and sifted through patients' files in a certain way. There was only one difference I could see. It was the way Given held his hands open – an honest and empathetic sort of gesture. It wasn't for anything specific, but was just his general posture. It reminded me of when he'd found me in the forest – open and calm palms.

Erin and Madam roamed around the room, giving out water and taking down notes on charts the people carried with them. I went back to stirring the cookie dough but snuck peeks whenever I could. The day merged into evening too quickly for my taste, but soon, the clinic was closed, and Given and Janie were packing up to leave. Given zipped up his red duffle bag filled with medical supplies, and I followed him out the door to where Janie was loading up the SUV. Erin had trailed behind me, gripping my shoulders playfully as he did. Madam and Bobby had said their goodbyes inside the manor. According to Erin, he and I were the send-off party.

"We'll be back soon," Janie promised. "Before you even have time to miss us."

I shrugged, knowing that wasn't possible, because they hadn't even left, and I already missed them. Janie and Given brought a lightness to the manor that I'd never felt before. Janie was always laughing and smiling as she told stories of their adventures. She reminded me of Bobby, but less weighed down, more carefree. Given was always Given, a new breed of human in a way.

"I'll be counting the hours, hon, until I see your precious face again," Janie said, pulling me into a hug. For once, my limbs didn't tighten up with awkwardness.

"Bye," I whispered, gripping her more tightly.

"Goodbye," she said, giving me one last squeeze.

Given was hugging Erin as Janie sashayed up to them.

Janie chuckled. "Switch."

"Take care, kid," Erin said, patting him on the back.

"You too," Given said.

"You're good with people," I said as Given approached me.

"That's an interesting goodbye." Given laughed. "Well, you're very sweet."

"I mean it. You just have this way, like you understand them. Never mind," I mumbled, wilting my head toward the dirt.

"I meant what I said, too. You have this intriguing adorableness about you."

"Well," I said, clearing my throat, "see you soon?"

He nodded. "Until then, Fair Maiden," he said with a gentlemanly bow.

"Come on, Given. Hug the girl and get your hide inside," Janie said from the driver's seat, emphasizing her statement with a honk of her horn.

Given enfolded me in his arms, pulling me tightly to him. An overwhelming scent filled my nose as my cheek pressed against his shoulder. It was a sharp, soapy fragrance mixed with some sort of plant, like aloe.

"See you soon," he whispered into my hair, and then his arms were gone as he leaped into the SUV, leaving butterflies to flap inside my stomach in his absence.

Twenty-five

Out in the catching field, I took a deep breath, trying to smell rain, but there was no trace. I was high up on one of the catcher platforms, fixing an electrical grid that had malfunctioned. As I slipped the screwdriver back into my tool belt, I pulled out a wrench. I closed up the metal box covering, sealing up the mechanical workings of the electrical grid and tightened the screws to keep the rain out. The metal was weather-beaten, but I thought it should hold up for the rest of the season.

"Hey, up there!"

I peered down to see who had called up to me. To my surprise, Given was gazing at me with a bright, beaming smile. My stomach became overpopulated with frantically flapping butterflies.

"Hi!" I shouted, giving a quick wave.

I flipped the switch, and the electrical grid hummed to life. Once I had climbed down the wooden pole, I looked up at Given, who stood next to Erin. I could never get used to seeing

Given's eyes. The intriguing, extraterrestrial silver seemed to make the butterflies flap more wildly inside my stomach. It was the best and worst thing in the world. My cheeks heated with the commotion inside my stomach, and I looked down and stared at his boots and my sneakers.

"You're early," Erin said thoughtfully. "Really early."

I looked up, realizing that we had just said goodbye to them a few weeks ago; they weren't due back for at least another week.

"Just passing through, actually," Given said with a sheepish smile. "Hope you don't mind. We heard that they needed help in territory one-fourteen. We thought we'd drop by and say hi."

Erin laughed. "And get a bed for the night?"

"Better than sleeping in the SUV," Given said, his coy smile widening. "We come bearing gifts, if that helps our case any."

Erin slapped Given on his back saying, "You know you're always welcome here, Given, but gifts are a good tool for sucking up."

Their laughter mingled together, drifting on the chilly wind toward me, tugging at my lips, begging me to join them.

"How long are you staying?" I asked.

"Just for the night," Given said.

"Oh," I whispered, trying to keep disappointment out of my voice.

"Well, we were just doing some quick repairs before we head off to Gina's," Erin said.

"Gina's?" Given questioned.

"Oh, that's right. You've never met her. She's our mechanic. Betsy needs to see the doctor."

"You mind if I come?" he asked, a giant, persuasive grin pinned to his face.

"I don't care, but it's not just up to me," Erin said and glanced over at me. "It's kind of our thing, so you'd have to ask her, too."

"Basil." Given turned and stared at me straight on with his enticing, silver eyes. "Is it all right if I intrude on your trip with Erin?"

"Well..." I said, one corner of my lips perking up.

Given smiled sweetly at me. "Please"

I laughed. "Umm..."

"You're so enjoying seeing me squirm."

"It's a perk," I admitted with a giggle.

Erin egged me on. "Make him beg."

"No, no, you don't have to beg. It's okay if you come."

"Okay, let's wash up and head out," Erin said, clapping his hands together.

*

After we washed up and said hi to Janie, the three of us loaded into Betsy and headed off to Gina's. Erin drove, Given sat in the back, and I sat in my usual passenger's seat. Given and I passed his notebook back and forth, playing tic-tac-toe until Betsy's tires crunched on Gina's driveway. Erin did the secret Gina honk, which probably wasn't so secret if Given knew now.

Gina shuffled out and up to our window. Ever since Oddy had been taken, Gina hadn't been the same. The corners of her lips always faced the ground, and her cheeks were sunken with sadness. Gina scarcely looked like herself anymore.

"I know I'm early, but Betsy really needs to see the doc," Erin said, leaning out of his window.

"Pull into the garage and let me take a look," Gina said, marching away.

My heart hurt so much for her and for Oddy. Wondering what had happened to Oddy, I knotted my fingers tightly together, twisting the ends of my sweater with my fidgeting. Erin pulled into Gina's makeshift garage.

"Everything alright?" Given asked, tapping me on my shoulder.

"Yes," I said, rubbing my temple, which had begun to pulsate more viciously. "Is it alright if I wait up at the house?" I asked Gina as I stepped out of the Bronco.

"Sure," Gina said, popping open the hood and burying her body underneath it.

Leaving Given and Erin behind, I headed out of the garage to the small dirt path that took me into Gina's junkyard. The farther I got from Gina's garage, the better I felt. It was too hard to stay in the auto body shop; I felt too guilty. I gazed at the old, rusted cars of the junkyard, lingering in each of my steps, not really wanting to reach Gina's house. I stopped halfway between the house and the garage. I looked back and forth, only able to see the tops of the buildings past the heap of cars, not sure which way to go. I finally took a seat on a stack of tires that looked in decent enough condition. Not knowing what else to do with myself, I started to examine the junkyard, something I'd never really taken the time to do. I stared at a license plate of an old Thunderbird. It was mostly in one piece, and it wasn't as weather-beaten as the others. Less than half of the license plate was legible. Cali 62W, it read.

I took in a few more faded license plates and a few more rusted, ivy-covered cars before I dropped my face into my hands, taking deep breaths, thinking about Gina, about Oddy, and about how I'd gotten into this mess. Suddenly, my stomach started to churn, and heat began to fill my forearm. I pressed it close to my chest, looking over at Gina's auto body shop as fear trickled into my body. Then I heard a low, rumbling growl, something in between animal and mechanical. I looked towards Gina's house, and there, standing in the middle of the dirt path was a machine—a wolf. My heart lurched, feeling as if it were caught somewhere in my throat. The wolf had a metallic coat, and it straddled the dirt as if it were ready to pounce. I had never seen a wolf before; I only knew about them through books and Madam's science lessons. Even still, I knew this had been manufactured to look like one. It gave another mechanical snarl, and my heart thudded even harder. It stepped cautiously toward me, not too slow, but not too fast. The closer it got, the more my arm burned and my stomach churned. As the wolf skulked into the sun, fear seeped further into me, penetrating my bones. The wolf's eyes were cold and robotic, resting inside its skull lifelessly, black lenses like that of a vid-recorder.

The fire crawled up my arm, and I knew I didn't have much time before the pain became debilitating. I did the only thing I could think of doing; I lunged for the rusted Thunderbird. I slipped into the driver's seat through the open window. The wolf growled heatedly as I scrambled to the backseat and crawled out of the shattered rear window. I jumped into the back of some hatchback, which had no trunk door, and climbed over the seats and crawled through the passenger's side window, landing in the bed of a truck. I squeezed through the tiny back window, falling into the cab, and I could hear the wolf scratching its way out of the hatchback and onto the bed of the truck.

I looked around, but all the windows were rolled up. The passenger side door panel was nothing but shreds of fabric and scrap metal. I yanked on the handle, but it broke in my hand.

The wolf was at the window, trying with all its might to push its way in, but it was too big for the small window. I pushed myself up against the door, trying to stay out of the wolf's reach, and slammed my body against the door, hoping my weight would pop it open, but after a few painful tries, I knew it wasn't going to work. The handle for the manual window on the driver's side looked strong enough to be used, or maybe I was just hoping it was strong enough because it was my only option. The wolf had almost half its body inside the cab. I slid down onto the floorboards of the truck and skidded toward the other side. The wolf became wilder as I slid in front of it and hit the steering wheel as the mechanical animal tried to force the rest of its body past the window. To my surprise, the horn worked and filled the inside of the cab with ferocious bursts of noise.

I stretched out my hand and pulled the handle down with my fingertips. As the window opened a slit, hope filled my muscles. I pushed the handle up and then down again until the gap was wide enough for me to get through. I stood, keeping as much of my body against the door as I could, but the wolf suddenly broke free and charged at me, forcing backwards out of the truck. I fell onto the soft, fabric hood of a convertible that had been swallowed by ivy. The wolf jumped through the window of the truck and landed gracefully in front of me. I screamed; my voice felt scratchy like I had been screaming all this time without even knowing it.

I started to crawl backwards as the wolf strutted forward. All of a sudden, there was a loud ripping noise, and the roof broke out from under me. I dropped onto a leather driver's seat. As I clawed at the ivy that encompassed me, I crawled to the backseat, searching for another escape, but there was nothing.

Heat consumed my arm and poisoned my stomach. I pulled up my sweater, and the darkness in the convertible was gone. The leather seats were splashed in a bright, golden-yellow light that emanated from my forearm.

"Basil!" Erin shouted off in the distance.

Given's voice followed next.

I wanted to call out to them, but my vocal cords wouldn't work. My heart hammered so savagely inside my chest that I just sat waiting for my ribs to start breaking. The wolf climbed into the car and leapt for me. I pushed my back hard against the seat and squeezed my eyes closed, waiting for it to strike.

When nothing happened, I opened my eyes a sliver. The wolf stood still in front of me. I stared curiously at it, clutching my beaming arm. The metal animal seemed pacified in a way. Maybe it was because my stomach felt slightly better; the burning in my arm had started to quell; my heart was slowing down; and my fear wasn't as ruthless. Then, out of nowhere, white light exploded inside my brain as the fire rushed up my arm, consuming my neck and cheek with heat.

I clutched my head with one hand and dug my fingers into the leather seat with the other. A wild, crude scream clawed its way out of my throat. There was something different about the explosion in my brain. It felt more penetrating, more meticulous. It felt as if there was something inside my head crawling around and pulling at file folios that were my memories. My brain felt scrambled, confusing my thoughts. I struggled forward, but the wolf nudged me back with its head.

I clutched my head with both my hands as my mind filled with a memory of Oddy. I was lying on Oddy's bed as she made shadow puppets on the wall. She called it Shadow Creature Theater, mostly because she couldn't make shadow puppets that looked like anything. The only thing she could do well was a bunny, and that was usually the main character of her plays: Edgar, the bunny. This particular play was when Edger was hopping through the forest and met an alien creature. Even now I could hear Oddy's laughter bounce off the wall as Allen the alien and Edger the bunny played hide and seek. Tears filled my eyes as Oddy bobbed up and down cheerfully on the bed in my mind. I remembered her knee jabbing uncomfortably into my rib. I almost laughed, because I was curled up on the backseat of a car that was nothing better than scrap metal, in excruciating pain, and that was what I remembered: being uncomfortable. I threw out my hand and struggled to push the wolf away by its muzzle. It shook my hand off, and I fell forward onto the floor.

"Basil." A deep, booming voice pierced its way into my chaotic mind. "Get away from her!"

The wolf snarled as it was jerked away from me. My mind went blank as the wolf clawed its way out of the car through the plastic rear window. My arm still flamed, and my brain felt like mush.

"Basil," the man said again as he struggled to squeeze into the car. "Oh, my goodness." He gasped as he clutched my arm, which still glowed like a beacon in the dark.

I lifted my head and saw a brawny man with a lot of wrinkles. I yanked my arm out of his grip, screaming. As soon as I got loose, I scurried backwards onto the seat, pushing my back into the cushion.

"It's me, Basil. Erin. Everything is going to be okay," he said, grasping my tiny frame.

My limbs were too weak to fight his strong grip. The man pulled down the arm of my sweater just before he pulled me toward the hole in the roof. Two warm, sturdy arms wrapped around me.

"You got her, Given?"

"Yeah," a much younger, calmer voice said.

The boy pulled me out of the car and helped me to a sturdy spot on the car's hood. He sat me down, and my head lolled toward the expanse of rusted metal on which I now sat.

"Basil?" His voice was smooth and syrupy-sweet, like honey.

Everything was spinning, and my stomach still churned. I tried to pull away from this boy I didn't know. My muscles turned to liquid for a few short seconds, and I fell backwards. The boy caught me and sat me back up. He ripped open a hole in the arm of my sweater and pressed a gray wad of fabric onto a cut that was underneath.

"Basil, are you okay?" he asked, pressing his hand to my cheek.

I jerked my face away from his inviting palm.

"Basil?" He sounded confused. "What happened?" He grasped my elbow and dabbed at my cut.

I pushed away from him, sliding off the hood of the convertible and into the bed of a truck. My fall was cushioned by ivy and foliage. The boy rushed over to me, pulling me up. I pushed his warm hands off me, feeling sobs clog my throat, unable to escape.

"Is she alright?" the older man asked frantically.

"It's me, Given," the boy said, taking a step toward me. "Please, just say something."

I stumbled backwards, knocking against the side of the truck's bed. I almost fell over, but the boy's arms tangled around my frame, entwining me in an inescapable cocoon. Before I could do anything, he pressed me close to his chest, stroking my hair as he did. He smelled of soap and aloe, a strong and familiar fragrance.

"It's okay. Everything's okay," he whispered, holding me tightly.

He placed his hand on my cheek and pulled my face to his. Then I saw them: silver irises that radiated solace. It was his captivating, extraterrestrial eyes that helped me push past the murkiness of my mind—so unique, so memorable, so innately woven into my consciousness.

"Given?" I choked out.

He pressed his forehead to mine. "It's okay. It's okay. You're okay," he repeated, as if he needed to convince himself.

"Given," I whispered slowly, feeling the familiarity of his name slide off my tongue.

"What was that?" he questioned.

I shook my head against his. With his fingertips, Given wiped at the tears that streaked down my cheeks, ones I didn't know had escaped.

"I don't know what that thing was," Erin said, stepping closer to us. "Let's just get back to the garage. I don't think it's coming back, but I don't want to wait around to find out."

Given helped me steady myself. I soon realized I was far from the dirt path, surrounded by rows of cars parked bumper to bumper. I wondered how they'd found me in all this mess. Given and Erin helped me climb my way back to the dirt path, and I fell to my hands and knees as my insides crawled up my throat and fertilized the dirt under me. They helped me to Gina's garage, holding me up with their shoulders under my arms.

Given loaded me into the backseat of the Bronco as Erin got the keys from Gina and explained what had happened. Erin ended with an offer for her to come with us, but she strongly declined. Given dug through the glove compartment and found the small first-aid kit Erin had stashed away years ago. I pulled my seatbelt across my body, but my hands were shaking so much that I kept missing the hole to lock it. Given cupped my hands in his and helped me secure it in place.

"How are you feeling?" he asked, his voice laced with an extra coat of molasses.

"Peachy," I coughed out, the word reminding me of Bobby.

"Basil," Given jeered, his composure faltering slightly. He cleared his throat, and his face was calm again. "On a scale from one to ten, ten being the worst pain you've ever felt and one being no pain at all, how bad?"

"Umm," I said, feeling the pain in my body start to settle down.

I heard fabric ripping as Given tugged on the tear in my sweater, exposing my battered arm. He ripped open an alcohol pad and dabbed it across my cuts. It burned a little, but nothing like what I had felt consuming my other arm.

"Everyone buckled?" Erin asked, sliding into the driver's seat and starting Betsy up.

"Yeah," Given said, placing a gauze pad on the biggest gash.

"I'm sorry," I whispered.

"What?" Given asked, looking at me with sad eyes. The silver had turned to a gloomy, molten color. I'd never seen him look so sad before. He cleared his throat, and the sadness was gone. "Why are you sorry? You have nothing to apologize for."

"For scaring you," I whispered.

He chuckled awkwardly. "It takes a lot more than this to scare me. Sorry, Fair Maiden. You'll have to try harder next time." He gave me one of his half-cocked smiles.

"Oh, okay," I said, leaning my head against the seat and closing my eyes.

I wondered if he knew I didn't believe him.

Twenty-Six

I woke up on the couch in the living room. It was dark, aside from the light that filtered in through the hallway. My heart lurched, fearing it was early morning and Janie and Given had left before I'd had a chance to say goodbye. I was wrapped burrito-style in my cream throw blanket. As I sat up, my head pounded dully. I got up and headed toward the lit hallway. A mixture of laughter bounced off the walls as I moseyed into the dining room. Erin, Madam, Bobby, Janie, and Given were all sitting around the table, which was covered with clothes and a half-filled box. Janie was holding up a red, slightly dingy button-up shirt to Madam.

"Oh, yeah, so your color," she said.

"Hey, Baze," Erin said, pushing out the seat next to him. "How're you feeling?"

I sat down next to him. "Good."

"I brought something for you, too," Janie said to me, sounding excited. "See, now that I know you actually exist, I can pick out clothes just for you." Janie squealed as she dug through the cardboard box.

I looked down at the clothes I was wearing, wondering whom they were originally intended for. My jeans always hung loosely off my hips, and the legs were always hemmed several inches at the bottom. Madam always altered my shirts, tailoring them just enough to fit.

"I hope you like it," Janie said, pulling out a lacy, light blue ball of fabric.

As she unfolded the lace atop the table, a dress started to take form. It was of white lace overlapping dark blue cotton. The combination made it appear light blue, as I had originally seen. The sleeves were short, and the white lace was cut in a loose V-neck to reveal the dark blue. It was lovely, delicate, and completely impractical.

"Well?" Janie asked, as she tried to flatten the wrinkles with her hands.

"Umm," I said, fingering the lacy skirt as my cheeks flushed.

"I thought you could wear it when the weather starts to heat up." Janie smiled.

"It's beautiful," I whispered.

"You're so adorable; I just thought you should have something to match," Janie said, picking up the dress and holding it in front of me.

I looked down, touching the lace as if I were wearing it.

"You should try it on."

"Umm," I stammered, "maybe later."

"Please," Janie persisted.

"Thank you so much, Janie. How about I'll try it on before you leave?" I said with a small, pleading smile.

"Oh, alright," she said, pressing her hand to my cheek for a quick second.

"Oh!" Bobby shouted, slapping his hand to his forehead. "I'm gonna need some help with tonight's dinner."

"What time is it?" I asked.

"It's—" Madam trailed off as she looked out to the grandfather clock in the hallway. "—five forty-three. Oh, it's past dinner time."

"It'll be okay, Maggs," Erin said, patting her hand. "Things can wait till tomorrow."

"But—"

"No buts. Everyone deserves a night off."

"Erin," Madam said, looking worried.

"Maggie." Erin turned to her and just looked at her, seeming to tell her something through his intense stare.

I glanced over at Given, thinking about the effect his silver eyes had on me. Maybe I was more like Madam than I realized, or maybe that was how you knew you understood someone, when their eyes told you more than what they said out loud.

Madam's shoulders eased as she whispered, "Okay."

"Great!" Bobby said, jumping up, "Basil, Given, you've been recruited. Kitchen. Pronto."

I left the dress with Janie and my throw blanket with Erin as I marched into the kitchen.

"What's going on, Bobby?" Given asked, stepping into the kitchen behind me.

"I'm making something special for everybody, but I have a few more orders to do. Soooo," Bobby lingered in the middle his sentence.

"So you want us to make it?" I asked.

"And Bingo was his name-o," Bobby said.

171

"What is it?" I asked.

He held up an index finger and pranced over to the refrigerator. After digging around for a couple of seconds, he emerged holding an armload of vegetables.

"Where did you get all these?" I asked.

Bobby laughed. "I could tell you, but then I'd have to kill you." He laughed some more and looked over at Given. "It helps to know the right people."

"You?" I asked, pointing at Given.

"I know a guy," he said with a shrug.

"I wanted to make my special vegetable soup," Bobby said, sorting the vegetables.

My mouth watered at the sight of lush carrots, zucchini and yellow squash, cauliflower, red potatoes, celery, and onions. Bobby pulled out a can of chicken broth, a small, white tub, and a piece of paper caked in food stains.

"I started making it but only got as far as finishing my special tomato sauce," Bobby said, placing his hand on the small, white tub. "Now, before I bestow upon you two the recipe for making this delicious soup, you must promise not to speak a word of this to anyone." Bobby grabbed the piece of paper that was stained with food and pressed it to his chest. "Or you run the risk of having your taste buds plucked off your tongue."

"Your secret is safe with me," I said.

"My lips are sealed," Given promised, running his fingers across his lips as if he were zipping them shut. He locked them closed and handed me the "key."

"Okay," Bobby said, handing me the recipe. "I'll be watching,"

Twenty-Seven

"It says sauté the onions," Given teased, raising one of his eyebrows at me.

"I am sautéing them," I said confidently.

"No, not sear. Ssssaaauuutttéeee," he taunted me.

"Just pay attention to what you're chopping and leave the onions to me," I jeered, trying to block his view of the pot with my body.

"You have to move them around more, or you're going to burn them."

"Stop backseat cooking."

"If I don't, we are going to end up with burnt onions, and then where will we be?"

"Do you want to sauté the onions?" I asked, pointing the wooden spoon at him.

"Yeah," Given said, reaching for the spoon.

"No," I said, whipping it out of his grasp. "I know what I'm doing."

"Why give me the option if you're not going to let me do it anyway?"

"You're supposed to be a gentleman and refuse, but I guess that was a long shot, being that you aren't one," I said, swiftly turning around and stirring the onions.

"Oh, ouch!" Given coughed out a laugh as he approached me. "What happened to, 'You're good with people'?"

My cheeks flushed as I stirred the onions again. "If you're going to throw my own words at me, then I'll stop being nice to you."

"Bah!" He laughed. "You? Be mean? You're too sweet for that."

"That's what you think," I said, putting my hands on my hips and narrowing my eyes at him.

"Oh, I'm withering from your stare. Make the pain stop." He bumped my hip with his, making me stumble sideways a step. "I think some of them are burning."

"Back away from my onions," I said, pointing the wooden spoon at him.

"Whoa, Basil. I'm just thinking of everyone here," Given said, holding up his hands in a surrendering gesture.

"Don't make me use this," I said, taking a step closer to him. "I banish you from my stovetop."

"Your stovetop?" Bobby said.

"Bobby's stovetop. I banish you from Bobby's stovetop that he is so generously letting me use."

"Butter is better," Bobby said, giving me an approving nod.

"You banish me?" Given repeated.

"Yes," I said, crossing my arms and standing on my tippy toes, trying and failing to make myself as tall as him. "Go." He

174

opened his mouth in protest, but I put my index finger to my lips. "Shhh, pretty things shouldn't talk."

His mouth snapped shut, but one of the corners of his lips shot up toward the ceiling in that half-cocked smile.

"Oh, so I'm pretty now?" Given chuckled.

"I was being sarcastic."

I was laughing so hard that my side started to hurt.

"You win this round," Given pushed through his own fit of laughter.

I shot Given a wide, pleased smile, which only made him laugh harder. I felt triumphant as Given swayed over to his countertop.

"You're just lucky we don't need any Basil in this soup," Given said. "Then we'd have to chop you up, because we don't have any."

"Eww," Bobby said, grimacing down at his bowl of cake batter.

"That doesn't make any sense," I said, shooting him a scowl. "And here I thought you were smart."

"I am smart. Basil, you. Basil, herb. It makes perfect sense." He tossed pieces of zucchini into the big bowl of vegetables. "Ha ha. I think it's hilarious. Ha ha ha."

Bobby laughed so hard he knocked the spatula out of his bowl. Given quickly snatched it from midair, moving faster than I'd seen anyone move. When Given looked up at us with cake batter splattered across his face and shirt, our roaring laughter started all over again.

"Mmmm," he said, licking the batter off his lips.

I chuckled. "I guess your catlike reflexes aren't that great."

"I meant to do that."

"I'm so, so sorry, Spatuly," Bobby said, grabbing the spatula out of Given's hands.

As our laughter died down, I added the chicken broth and Bobby's special tomato sauce. We tossed in all the vegetables, and sat on the stools, playing tic-tac-toe as we watched the soup simmer.

"Hey, I have something for you," Given said, patting down the many pockets of his khaki cargo pants.

"Oh," I said, caught off-guard. "You didn't have to."

"I saw it when my mom was trading for clothes," he said, pulling something out of his side zipper pocket. "For you." He held out his hand as a small yellow-and-gray-striped sweatband rested on his palm.

I looked down at my dark green sweatband and felt my heart skip several beats. I clasped my hands together on top of the bar table.

"I noticed your green one and thought you might like it," he said, placing it on top of our game of tic-tac-toe.

"Thanks," I whispered, still not meeting his gaze.

"It looks kind of small," Given said, picking it back up and stretching it out. "You should try it on and see if it fits. If it doesn't, then I'll trade for another."

I ran my fingers over my sweatband, the one I'd been wearing for as long as I could remember, and then looked over at Bobby to find him staring intently at me. It wasn't the fix of his gaze that took me by surprise. It was his small, reassuring smile that did. Bobby gave me a small nod and turned his attention back to his order. It was as if Bobby thought I should tell Given about my etching. I wanted to confide in Given, but years of hiding made the idea seem crazy. I couldn't tell him, could I? I glanced at his smooth, clean forearms, wondering how I could explain this to him.

"Are you okay, Basil?" he asked, trying to capture my gaze with his eyes.

"Yes." I looked up at him and trying to smile, but my lips pressed into an awkward grin instead.

"I mean okay-okay." He narrowed his eyes in a probing kind of way.

My eyes darted down and up again. "See? Even my eyes are saying yes." I managed to soften my smile, and then looked at him more seriously. "I'm okay-okay. Okay?"

Given took a breath and frowned at the yellow and gray sweatband. He fiddled with it mechanically, stretching it out with his fingers a couple of times.

"We lost you for a second," he whispered, making it sound more like a confession.

"What?" I asked.

"When we found you in the junkyard, you didn't recognize me." His voice held a hurtful ping in it.

I laced my fingers tightly together, not wanting to be pulled back to that moment, because he was right. The whole incident had scared me so much that my fear-o-meter couldn't register that high. Within seconds, I was nine years old again, not knowing a thing about myself.

"I know." I bit my lip, gripping my fingers tighter.

"That scared me the most," Given said, taking a staggered breath. "More than..." His voice drifted as he gazed down at my bandaged arm.

"Me too," I admitted and then turned my gaze to our game of tic-tac-toe.

When I finally looked up at Given, he was still gaping at my bandaged arm. The fix of his stare was somewhere between protective and anxious. I poked his hand with my index finger. As his eyes met mine, they melted into a soft pool of liquid silver. He gave me one of his famous half-cocked smiles. I looked back over at Bobby, who glanced my way and rolled his eyes at me. I took a breath, trying not to act cowardly, trying to be bold, and trying to let him in.

"I have a…" My voice trailed off. I couldn't speak. Fear of how he would react made every way of telling him seem not good enough.

"You have a what?" Given prompted.

I took a gulp of air as painful silence filled the space separating us. Gnawing on my lip, I thought back to just a few minutes ago, when we had laughed back and forth with each other in such a carefree way. I wanted to rewind time and stay in that moment forever, with Given giving me his half-cocked smile as his silver eyes flickered with mischievousness.

"Basil," he said as he placed two of his fingers in my hand, reminding me of when we'd first met, back when his existence was scary but intriguing to me. I guess things had always been bizarre and unusual between us. With my eyes, I followed his fingers up his tanned arm to his sturdy shoulder, his sharp cheek, and then rested my gaze on his calm, silver eyes. They were still extraordinary to me, alien and captivating. I turned on my stool and placed my arm in front of him. Given broke our gaze and looked down at my sweatband.

"Befo—" I started but couldn't finish. I wanted to give him some kind of warning, something to help him prepare, but my voice dried and died inside my mouth.

Like peeling skin from bone, I pulled my sweatband away from my etching. I'd never felt more exposed than I did at that moment, and what made it worse was that I couldn't decipher Given's expression. His eyes became focused and transfixed on my sleek pucker of skin. He skimmed his index finger along a solitary line of deep scar tissue. He didn't look horrified or worried. His face was relaxed and collected.

"Madam and Erin aren't my real parents. They found me alone in a swamp a long time ago. I can't remember anything before that. I don't know my name or where I came from. I don't even know if I'm actually seventeen. I've never met any other kids except Od—" I stopped short as sadness sank into me. I wanted to rip my arm away, to push all of these sad realities away. Tears started to clog my throat. I looked down at the tile floor. "I've never met anyone close to my age before." I took a gulp of air. "I've never shown anyone my...my arm before."

"You've been hiding all this time?" Given asked, letting my arm go.

"Up until recently, I've never really looked at it like that, but I guess—" I cradled my etched arm with my other, watching it as if it were a tentacle of some kind of wild creature. "I guess I have been. I wanted to tell you. I...I...j-j-just," I stuttered nervously, shaking my head back and forth. I kept my eyes trained on my etching, as if I were waiting for the creature to strike. "There are no words to describe this, Given." The tears in my throat made it hard to push my voice out. It coated everything in a shy quiver.

"I understand," he said softly.

I looked up at him, and his eyes told me that he meant it. I studied his face more closely, at the sharpness of his features

179

conflicting with the softness of his eyes. Then I noticed something strange. It was small and practically invisible, but tucked inside the corner of his lips was a hint of a smile. It was so tiny I thought I might have been imagining it.

"You're not scared?" I asked, recalling Madam's and Erin's reactions when they'd first seen my forearm.

He shrugged nonchalantly. "No."

"You know what this is, right?" I asked, holding out my etched arm for him to take another look, as if he had missed something the first time.

"Yes."

"You know that I've been etched," I said more forcefully.

Given's eyebrows furrowed. "Is that what they call it over here?"

"What?"

"Every territory calls it something different – tagged, stained, scared, marked, selected, chosen. When you've been etched, that's when they come for you. That's why there aren't a lot of kids around. Yes, Basil, I know what it means. Why are you acting like you expect me to run out of this room screaming?"

"I..." my eyes grew wide as I somehow drifted onto foreign ground. Given wasn't like anyone I've ever met before. Maybe, somewhere inside of me, I expected him to completely reject me, to be so horrified of me, more than anyone else, because wasn't he at risk of being taken too? "Gina's daughter, Oddy, is gone because of me."

"You can't honestly think that," Given said, "because if that were true, wouldn't they have taken you, too?"

"I don't know," I said, curling my shoulders forward timidly. "I guess."

"It's not your fault, Basil." He took a deep breath, running a hand through his hair reflexively, and then he pulled out the necklace that he kept tucked inside his shirt. Silence lingered between us as he turned the rectangular prism over in his hand. He took another deep breath. "Does this look familiar to you?"

"Yes," I said, looking at the small metal prism in his fingertips, wondering how he knew.

He huffed slightly and ran his thumb against the smooth metal, staring at it intensely.

"You asked me once," Given said, looking up at me, "if we'd ever met before now."

"Yes."

Letting the prism drop and rest against his gray t-shirt, Given looked up at me in a probing kind of way. His eyes were searching for something, something that seemed hidden somewhere along my cheeks and in my eyes.

"We have." He narrowed his eyes inquisitively. "It's just..." His voice trailed off as he got up from his seat and marched around the bar table.

"It's just what?" I asked, standing up and pressing my hands on the tabletop.

Abruptly stopping in front of the sink, Given looked over at me. "Do you remember me? I mean...really remember me?" There was a strange hitch in his voice.

"I don't know," I said with a meek voice that held a lot of uncertainty. "Maybe. A figure really." I took a gulp. "I think."

Given dropped his head and took another sharp breath in. It was awkwardly quiet for a second or two. Then he snapped his head back up with determined eyes. "Basil, I need to tell you something."

"What is it?" I asked.

"Wow!" Janie's voice broke into the room unexpectedly. "It smells so good in here."

I quickly grabbed the closest sweatband, which was Given's, and covered my etching. The striped yellow-and-gray sweatband fit more snugly around my arm than my green one ever had.

"I think it's done," Given said, grabbing the wooden spoon and stirring the soup.

"Oh good," said Janie, pressing her hand to her stomach and licking her lips. "I'm starving."

Twenty-Eight

"No," Madam opposed as she shook her head from side to side. "That is hardly proper."

"Come on, Maggie," Erin said, pulling Madam's arm through the hallway.

"You eat on a table, in a chair," she huffed.

"Dinner and a movie are what we all need right now," Erin said, moving his arm to Madam's back, practically dragging her toward the living room.

Given, Janie, and I followed silently behind them. A small smile crept across my lips as Erin lovingly forced Madam to slow down and rest for a bit. Madam paid Erin in wordless gratitude by constantly letting him win and letting her small hint of a smile touch the edge of her lips. When we wandered into the living room, Bobby was there to greet us with the pot of soup and a stack of bowls.

"Who's ready to watch a flick?" Bobby smiled, holding out an interweb vid-chip.

"How about we watch my movie?" Erin chimed in.

"You mean dust off your old VHS player?" Bobby chuckled until he met Erin's serious eyes, and then his laughter stopped.

"Yes," Erin said.

Bobby cleared his throat dramatically. "But this is new. Given and Janie picked it up for me. You might like it, Erin. Just give it a shot."

"No," he replied flatly.

"Please," Bobby said as nicely as he could.

"No."

"It might be good," I said with a small shrug.

Erin looked over at me, and with a deep, exaggerated exhale said, "Oh, alright. Upload it onto the screen."

"I knew we should have gone the adorable, squishy route from the get-go," Bobby said, snapping his fingers.

"Cuz Basil's just so marshmallowy sweet," Janie said, patting my shoulder.

I bit my lip and looked over at Given as my cheeks flushed. He gave me a wink.

"Okay," Bobby cheered, prancing up to the screen, and inserted the vid-chip into it. "Everybody grab some grub and take your seats. The flick is about to begin."

I poured myself a bowl of soup and curled up in the corner of the couch that my throw blanket had been draped over. Given took a seat at the opposite end of the couch, and Janie sat in-between us.

"Good job on the soup, guys," Bobby said, taking another spoonful. "Almost as good as I make it."

I looked over at Given, and we both shrugged and laughed at our sameness.

As the flick started, an old western town slowly came into focus. "When Jennifer found her way back home, it was a dawn of a new Wild West era," a male narrator said in a deep, dramatic voice as western music played in the background. "A western town in the middle of...the jungle."

"Oh, brother," Erin said, throwing up his hands.

"Shhhh," Bobby countered.

As the flick went on, I disliked it more and more. I didn't know if it had to do with the fact that the main character had forgotten how she'd gone missing or that there was something about her face that looked sad and defeated, but overall, the flick gave me a weird feeling.

"A polar bear in the jungle?" Erin coughed out through a laugh.

"Shhh," Bobby hissed. "it's vital to their dietary needs."

Erin burst into a fit of laughter. He had never been much of a fan of flicks. When I was younger and saw my first flick, Erin and Bobby started a big debate on what was better: flicks or movies. Erin would conclude his argument with how flick story lines were ridiculous, and how the graphics looked unrealistic. Bobby would conclude with how the sound and visual clarity were much better than on old VHS movies. Then Erin would bring up the old monster movies Bobby had a soft spot for, and the debate would start all over again. It was a vicious and hilarious cycle, one I'd seen only a handful of times.

As the night wore on, I drifted in and out of sleep, catching only bits and pieces of the flick. Pressure on the side of my leg startled me awake. My head jumped up from the armrest as I looked around the dimly lit living room. Bobby and Erin were on the floor cross-legged, watching Erin's old movie, having another helping of soup. They argued back and forth between mouthfuls of soup. Janie was curled up on the love seat, fast asleep. Given had stretched out asleep on the couch, pushing me further into the corner of the couch cushions. A deep yawn stretched out my lungs as I pushed Given's legs away from me. He rolled over in his sleep, pushing his face into the back of the couch. I stood up and covered him with my throw blanket and headed out of the living room.

"Night, kid," Erin said.

"Night, Baze," Bobby said quickly after, almost overlapping Erin.

"Night," I replied.

Twenty-Nine

I headed downstairs as the morning light lit the kitchen in a gloomy shade of gray. I poured myself a cup of coffee and sat down to watch Bobby knead a lump of dough. A large clatter came from the opposite side of the swinging door. I looked at Bobby; his eyebrows were raised with curiosity.

"Let's investigate," he said, and I jumped off my stool.

We pushed through the swinging door and padded down the hallway that led to the living room. When we reached the room, Janie and Given were running around frantically.

"Where are my shoes?" Janie asked, dropping her dark purple duffle bag by the entrance of the living room.

"I don't know. Where are mine?" Given said, digging around in his black bag.

"What's going on?" I asked.

"We overslept," Janie squeaked in horror. "We're going to be late."

Given pulled out a pair of socks and started to put them on, just as Janie found her boots. Given pulled off his gray thermal and threw it into his duffle bag. His metallic necklace rocked against his plain white t-shirt as he searched for his boots. Janie began to take inventory of what they had brought in with them.

"Is this everything?" she asked.

"Yeah, Mom," Given confirmed, pulling out his boots from underneath the couch.

"Are you sure?"

I scanned the room to see if they'd missed anything and noticed Janie's sweater pushed into the corner. I quickly picked it up and handed it to her.

"Thank you, honey," she said, touching my cheek. "Are you sure, Given?" Janie taunted him as she held up her sweater.

"You're making me look bad," Given told me, raising one of his eyebrows.

"You do that all on your own," I said with a coy smile.

"Oh, Basil, you have to promise me you'll show me that dress the next time we stop by," Janie said, shaking her finger at me.

"I promise, Janie."

I dropped to my knees in front of Given's black duffle bag. Half of his clothes were trying to make a break for it. I began pushing them back into his bag. Madam would cringe if she saw that his clothes were being packed unfolded.

"Thanks," he said as he helped me shove the clothes into his bag.

"You're welcome," I said, watching him zip up his bag.

Given laced up his boots as Janie dug around in her bag, making sure everything was there. I sat cross-legged on the floor, staring at Given's necklace and thinking of our conversation in the kitchen the night before.

"What is it?" he asked, lowering his face until he was in my line of sight.

"What?" I asked automatically, caught off-guard.

He laughed "You know, you're going to pull a brain muscle one of these days."

"Are you going to finish telling me what you were trying to tell me last night?"

"Oh," Given said, lifting up his eyebrows but not really seeming surprised by the question, as if he had been waiting for me to ask it.

"Is that a yes oh, or a no oh?" I asked, confused.

"It's a yes oh."

"Is this the kind of news I need to prepare for?" I grinned softly. "'Cuz knowing you, it could be a doozy."

Given chuckled nervously, and his cheeks turned slightly pink. "It's a secret I've never told anyone."

"So it is a secret." I smiled, feeling bold and nervous. Wings of butterflies fluttered against the walls of my stomach.

"Yes, it is."

"Okay, everything is here," Janie announced, zipping up her duffle bag. "Time to head out."

"The next time I come back, I promise to tell you," Given said, standing up and pulling the strap of his duffle bag across his chest.

"Okay." I looked down at my bare feet and his boot-covered toes.

All of a sudden, something brushed my neck, and then Given's rectangular prism came into view. I looked up just as he let the chain go. I grasped the prism, staring at the sleek metal and the three imprinted lines wrapped around the bottom.

"For collateral," Given said, closing my hand around the prism with his. "I promise, Basil." He let my hand go and pulled me into a hug goodbye. I drank up his cologne of soap and aloe.

Thirty

As always, when Given and Janie left, everything fell back into a normal pattern. I headed into the small mudroom after spending the entire day out with Erin in the catching field.

"What happened to you guys?" Bobby chuckled, peeking into the mudroom from the kitchen counter.

"One of the tarps broke," Erin said, digging mud out of his ear.

Both Erin and I were covered from head to toe in mud. As we'd been emptying out a tarp, we'd heard a loud, ripping noise, and soon, a torrent of water had crashed down on us.

"Let's just say there's a mini swamp out there," Erin said, pulling off his sweater.

I peeled off my own soaked sweater and rolled up my jeans.

"Oh, my goodness," Madam said from the doorframe.

She set down the stack of papers in her hands and started digging through the mudroom cabinets for towels.

"Use the downstairs washroom by the front door," she said, wrapping a towel around me. "Last thing I need are mud prints trailing up the stairs."

"You can go first, Basil," Erin said and then looked at Madam as she threw a towel around him. "I need to stay and kiss my wife."

I wrapped the towel around myself tighter as I headed out of the mudroom and into the kitchen.

"Erin, don't you dare," I heard Madam say as I grabbed one of the buckets of water that rested on the bar table.

"Aww, don't leave me, Maggs," Erin said.

"I have to get you and Basil some clean clothes unless you want to sleep outside." She made a beeline straight into the pantry as I pushed past the swinging door.

"I could make it work!" Erin yelled playfully.

I headed to the closest washroom, the one that was tucked under the giant staircase, and put the bucket inside the sink and pulled out a washcloth. I scrubbed my face first, and as I moved to my neck, I pulled off Given's and Oddy's necklaces, hanging them on one of the cabinet handles. A knock sounded at the door, and when I opened the door, Madam handed me some clean clothes. They were the pajamas Janie had picked out—green flannel pants and a black cotton tee. I finished washing as quickly as I could, because I knew Erin was waiting. As I strolled into the kitchen a few minutes later, I almost slipped on the wet floor.

"Careful," Madam said, dipping the mop into a pail of sudsy water.

"Erin, washroom is free!" I shouted out to him.

"Great," Erin said, tiptoeing through the kitchen, trying not to step on the clean, wet spots.

Madam quickly mopped the few mud prints Erin left behind. She then emptied the pile outside. "Okay," she said when she was finished. "Let's head to the library for your studies."

*

After studying and having dinner, I plopped onto my bed, exhausted. I turned onto my side, only having enough energy to drag my throw blanket, which had somehow made it back to my bed, over myself. The plush fabric seemed to be infused with Given's scent. Soap and aloe lulled me into sleep.

*

The sudden and frantic sound of honking startled me awake, dumping adrenaline instantly into my veins. I got up and headed down the pantry stairs, just as the honking stopped. There was a muffled, panicked conversation outside the swinging door, and then a dull, loud thud. As I pushed through the door, my stomach dropped, and my heart stopped. In the foyer, shaking and rattling against the hardwood floor was Given. Janie dropped down next to Given as Erin shut the door.

"What's going on?" Madam asked, rushing to Janie.

I quickly ran over to Given, dropping onto my knees at his side.

"I don't know," Janie said.

"What do you mean, you don't know?" Madam said.

"What happened to him?" I asked around the large ball of fear forming in my throat.

"I'm—" Given's hand moved to his stomach. "—okay." He gnashed his teeth together.

"I need a cold washcloth," Janie said.

"I'll get it," Madam replied, running out of the foyer.

Janie and Erin were speaking frantically back and forth, but their voices seemed to be getting farther away. My stomach churned viciously.

"Ssssokay," Given choked out, placing his hand on my cheek.

As his muscles twitched against my skin, I felt how feverishly hot he was. I pressed my hand to his forehead, and his skin scorched my palm.

"Ssssokay," Given said again as he pulled my hand away from his face.

"Here, Janie." Madam handed her a dripping washcloth.

Janie placed it on Given's forehead and then unzipped his sweater and pulled it off him.

"I'm o-o-k-kay," Given insisted, fighting to get up.

Between all the commotion and fear, I didn't realize that my forearm had started burning, but the sensation suddenly grew intense.

"Stay down, hon," Janie said sweetly.

"My s-s-st—" Given gulped. "My stomach."

My heart shuddered inside my chest, and I quickly grabbed Given's arm. I pulled up his black thermal and was greeted by a horrible golden-yellow light emanating from under the skin of his forearm. The room grew silent as they all stared at Given's glowing forearm.

"They found you?" I asked, letting go of his arm.

"No," Given said, shaking his head. "I've had this."

My hands started to shake as the burning crawled up my arm. I clasped my hands together in an effort to hide their trembling.

Struggling to sit up, he gripped his forearm. "This is m-m-my secret, Basil."

My stomach churned more ferociously. I tried so hard to hold onto my composure.

"This was what—" He stopped for a second and moved his hand to his upper arm. "—what I was trying to tell you. I'm sorry." Given stared up at me, his face racked with pain and fear, and reached up. "Basil?"

My body began to shudder so much that it became noticeable. Given jerked his hand back, as if he had infected me somehow.

"Basil?" Erin said, dropping to my side.

"We came here together," Given said, his body twitching from the pain. "You and me." He gritted his teeth as he balled his free hand. "They made us forget."

"Given. Stop," I choked out, wrapping my arms around my stomach. My body was beginning to warp from the flames in my arm.

"They erased everything. They took everything from us."

Erin pulled down my sweatband. My forearm blazed just as brightly as Given's. Madam gasped, and I stood up, feeling as if I needed to do something while I could still concentrate. Everyone gaped at me with shock painted across their faces. The walls felt like they were closing in on me, making it hard to breathe. My heart was thudding inside my chest.

"Basil, take it easy," Erin said, standing up in front of me.

My head was spinning, and having Given tell me that we had known each other even before I'd met Erin and Madam wasn't helping. Given was confusing me, and tears blurred my vision. The heat from my forearm crawled up and consumed my shoulder. It was happening so much faster than the other times. I stumbled away, pushing past Erin as I did, and staggered toward the washroom.

"Basil!" Erin called after me.

The burning quickly devoured my neck and cheek, setting off a supernova in my head. A loud scream left my lips as my body went limp. I thumped to the ground, feeling so raw, so confused, and so far away from my muscles. Loud, pounding footsteps approached me.

"Get the first aid kit!" Erin shouted, banging open the washroom door.

Madam scooped me up, and my body shook and trembled between her arms. My head jerked wildly as an old, forgotten memory crept in. I suddenly saw everything in an odd picture-in-picture kind of way.

I was running through the forest. The cold pricked my skin. Bobby came running up with the first aid kit. Given was running next to me, but he was a little boy. We were both kids, and we were running together.

Erin placed a freezing washcloth on my forehead; cold water ran down the sides of my face.

I heard growling coming from the trees in the woods, forcing adrenaline harder through my veins.

Janie rolled Given onto his side as he started to throw up.

As Given and I frantically ran through the forest, I felt a light tap against my chest; I looked down and saw a rectangular prism.

"She's burning up, Erin," Madam said, settling me alongside the claw-foot tub. The cold, tiled floor made my skin knit together.

Given and I ran into an old, decrepit house, trying to hide among the creaking wood.

"Press this onto her cheek," Erin said frantically, handing Madam a gauze pad from the first aid kit.

Everything was dark, except for the light beaming from both of our arms.

"Basil," Madam cooed in my ear, trying to pull me into the present.

I was suddenly jerked back, my necklace catching on something sticking out of the walls of the old house.

The contents of my stomach clawed up my throat, and I threw up on the gray tile of the washroom floor. Madam held me on my side until my gags turned to dry heaves. Erin threw down a towel as Madam wiped my face. I saw Given's necklace dangling alongside Oddy's on the handle of the cabinet. I had forgotten to put them back on after I cleaned up. The lines running around the bottom of the rectangular prism were strangely blinking white.

"Get ice!" Janie yelled, dragging Given into the washroom.

Erin and Bobby quickly ran to the kitchen.

"Let's get her into the tub," Janie said, rushing over to Madam.

Given's hand drifted into mine; both were limp and rattling with tremors. I could hear my heart in my ears, pounding loudly and quickly.

"Okay," Madam said, gripping me under my arms.

Janie clutched my legs. "One, two, three."

They heaved me up and gently placed me inside the claw-foot tub.

Given was at my side, trying to help me untangle my necklace.

Erin and Madam placed freezing bags of frozen dough and vegetables on top of me.

He helped me out of my necklace, and we left it behind.

I watched Given's rectangular prism hanging from the cabinet, swinging slowly back and forth.

In the mirror mounted above the sink, I could see Bobby and Janie packing frozen vegetables behind Given's neck and on his chest. All of a sudden, a deep, agonizing groan tumbled out of his mouth. Given gripped the bathtub and pressed his palm against his forehead. He rocked back and forth, making the frozen bags slide off his body.

The memory of Given and me in the forest soon faded away, and a different one took root. It clawed out from the back of my mind and exploded in my head. White filled my senses, and my breaths came in deep, panicked gasps. I drifted away from the porcelain of the tub and the alarm in the room, toward a memory of the time when everything in my life changed.

*

Blurry white. A blinding abyss of bleach. It was a strange white, and the air smelled of peroxide and antiseptic. My head was spinning, making everything dreamlike and bizarre. I lay on a gurney as people dressed in white from head to toe wheeled me through a long, echoing hallway. I saw bright florescent lights attached to an untarnished ceiling as they raced passed my face. The hallway felt endless, and so did the burning on my arm.

"The process has already started," someone above me said.

The people dressed in white looked creature-like in their stainless state. They gripped the gurney with rubber gloves. My eyes stung from all the white, as if one of these people—one of these creatures—had dumped bleach into them. Everything was so clean and new—the walls, the lights, their clothes. The burning started crawling up my arm, slow and steady. I blinked

198

up and saw one of the covered creatures staring at me. Its eyes gaped at me intensely, vivid green and ringed around the pupils.

The creatures pushed my gurney into a room that was just as white as the hallway, only there were stainless steel machines and another gurney. My heart shifted into high gear. Everything felt so foggy and surreal. The creature with the green eyes held up my arm; it was shining, bright, and yellowish gold. I looked over at the other gurney and saw a little boy. He looked over at me, and with all the bright lights in the room, it was easy to make out his intense silver eyes. The boy looked in pain, but he reached for me as if he knew me.

They wheeled my gurney to the opposite side of the room, and more creatures in white clothes surrounded me, so much so that I couldn't see the little boy past them. One of the creatures grabbed something that looked like a flashlight, then pulled my face towards his and ran it across my eyes. As the flashlight passed over my pupils, even more white overcame my vision. The light disoriented my senses and pulled me farther away from my appendages. Everything that was happening to me started registering in pieces as I wavered in and out of consciousness.

*

I roused into semiconsciousness to fingers sticking cold, metal probes onto my face. They were talking, but I was too far from my ears to hear what they were saying.

*

"Memory extraction is complete."

It was agonizing to try to hold onto consciousness. I tried to move my arms, but they just lay limp on the hard gurney.

"She's ready."

Icy hands prodded at my numb, empty body, pulling off wires and probes. I heard monitors beeping and buttons clicking.

*

Awareness drifted into me, and I was in a room with chairs pushed up against the walls. The metal chair I was sitting on didn't have any cushions, so I could feel the cold through my thin white pants. I heard the swish of a door opening, and a creature dressed in white marched in and knelt down in front of me; it was the creature with the green eyes. It looked from my right eye to my left several times and then placed a silver chain around my neck. On it was a rectangular prism.

My head was spinning, and I was having a hard time keeping myself upright. I pressed my hand to my forehead as a moan tumbled from my lips.

"Shhh." The creature cupped my mouth. "You're safe now."

It grabbed me and helped me to my feet. I took one shaky step, and then my limbs melted. I sank into the creatures arms, which wrapped around me and picked me up. The creature then carried me out of room.

Thirty-One

"I told you what happened to her arm at Gina's, Maggie. Why are you acting like I hid this from you?" Erin's voice was coated with frustration and worry.

Someone pulled off a bag of melted vegetables and replaced it with a frozen one.

"I just... I...I didn't," Madam stammered, searching for words she couldn't piece together. "You should have..." Madam took a gulp of air. "She shouldn't be glowing. That's not normal, Erin."

"I know it's not."

"Has this happened to Given before, Janie?" Madam asked in a tone verging on demanding.

"No," Janie replied.

I heard a groan followed by a few coughs.

"Given?" Janie cooed.

Bags of slushy vegetables plopped to the ground.

"How are you feeling, sweetie?"

"A three. I'm okay, Mom," Given wheezed out. "Basil." His voice spiked as he shot to a sitting position. "Whoa. Ouch."

"Are you okay?"

"Head rush. How's Basil?"

"Basil's okay," I said, cracking my eyes open to see everybody stare at me as if I were a glass doll. It made me nervous and embarrassed.

"How are you?" I asked Given.

"I'm fine."

"I'm sorry for scaring everybody," I said, biting my lip and curling my arms around myself.

"Oh, honey," Janie said, gripping my hand in hers. "You have nothing to apologize for."

"Here," Madam said, placing a towel under my head.

Janie put her hand on Given's forehead and brushed back his hair with her fingers. "Both your fevers broke just a few hours ago," she said, her voice full of relief.

"You think I'll make it?" Given joked weakly.

"I don't think you'll perish in the night," Janie's voice sounded too sad for it to be funny.

"I was just kidding, Mom," he said, putting his hand on her shoulder.

"I know. It's just…"

"It's just what?"

"Nothing," Janie said, shaking her head some more, and continued running her hand through Given's messy hair. "I'm just glad you're feeling better. Both of you," she added, glancing over at me.

Madam felt my forehead. When I looked up at her, she pulled her hand away and stormed out of the washroom. Erin quickly followed her.

"I'll be right back," Janie said, glancing at the spot where Erin and Madam were standing.

"I'll keep an eye on them," Bobby said from his awkward perch on the toilet, where he sat cross-legged and filled out paperwork.

Janie left partially open. Given lay back down on the tiled floor. The washroom grew quiet as soft whispers drifted through the cracked door. I grabbed the few bags of frozen vegetables and tossed them over the side of the tub, opposite of Given. I pulled at the towel that Madam slid under my head and clutched it in my arms as if it were a cozy pillow.

"Basil," Given whispered from behind the porcelain of the claw foot tub.

"Yes," I answered.

"How did you know?"

"Know what?"

"How did you know to look for my...etching?"

"You had all the..." My voice drifted away. I didn't know what to call it. "All the symptoms."

"Symptoms?" Given questioned. "What do you mean by that?"

"That's what happened to me when my etching—" I searched for the right words. "—did that."

"You mean this happened to you before?"

"Yes, a couple of times." I said, curling my legs in toward my stomach.

I could see Given in the mirror. A towel pillowed his head, and his hands rested on top of his chest. Surrounded by bags of sweating vegetables and mushy dough, he studied the white porcelain of the claw-foot tub as if he could see past it, as if he could see me curled up behind it.

"Given?" I broke the silence this time.

"Yeah?"

"I've seen your arm." I gulped. "It wasn't etched until now."

"It was." Given took a breath, letting it slowly escape past his lips. "I just hid it is all." He snuck a peek at me in the mirror, and I diverted my eyes to the lip of the tub. "You have a sweatband to cover yours; I have a spray to cover mine."

Silence swelled and lingered as I listened to his slow, even breaths.

"You know how you said we came here together?" I pressed my hand against the glossy wall of the tub, feeling my heart sputter in my chest. "How long have you known?"

"I think I've always known, in some way, that we had a past together," Given said, lightly tapping on the tub. "Most of my memories came back to me in dreams, but I've always carried around the one where we were running for our lives in the forest when we were younger."

"You looked familiar to me," I confessed. "You always had. I just didn't know why." I took a breath, trying to build up courage for my next question. "Why didn't you tell me?"

"Well—" Given took a gulp. "Why didn't you? Fear, shame, comfort—it was a mixture of things. Also, I didn't want to freak you out, because you didn't seem to remember me."

"Oh."

"You sort of beat me to it."

"So Janie's not your mom, is she?"

"No, but I love her all the same, and I know she loves me as if I were her real son."

I frowned. I'd never felt like I completely belonged with Erin and Madam. I never felt as if I was their adopted daughter.

"Hey," Given said, resting his hand on the lip of the tub. His fingers loomed over me a few inches from my face. "They love you. Don't doubt that."

"I know." A small smile crept across my lips.

"It turned out just right, you know?" Given said.

"What do you mean?"

"We were running through the forest and got split up somehow, but Janie found me, and Madam and Erin found you. We eventually found each other again."

"Yea, I guess, Mr. Silver Lining."

"Hey, it's better than letting it defeat you," he said, drumming his fingers on the porcelain.

My eyes drifted from his fingertips to watching him in the mirror. He was lying on one side, stretching his arm out awkwardly. Then I noticed something odd. His forearm was still glowing that bright, yellow-gold color. I looked down at my own forearm and realized mine looked the same.

"We're glowing," I said, quickly sitting up.

"Have we stopped?" Given asked calmly.

"You haven't," Bobby said, crouching down by the spout of the tub.

Given sat up, running his hand through his hair. He turned to Bobby. "How long have we've been out?"

"A day."

"And we haven't stopped glowing?" I asked as worry weeded its way around my words.

"No," Bobby said, shaking his head slowly.

I looked past Bobby, zeroing in on Given's necklace dangling alongside Oddy's. I stood up without thinking. Bobby and Given both stared up at me.

"Basil?" Bobby spoke first.

"Your necklace," I whispered as I climbed out of the tub and walked toward the cabinet.

"What is it?" Given asked, standing up.

I pulled the necklace off the knob and made my way out of the washroom. Bobby and Given followed me as I approached Erin, Madam, and Janie. The three of them were huddled around what looked like an old map. Half of it was in a very faded type, and the other half appeared to be hand drawn. I had never seen it before. It must have been Janie's.

"I don't know if it's safer to stay or le—" Erin himself off as his eyes shifted up. "Basil. Given."

"It's Given's necklace," I said, plopping it in the middle of their huddle.

"What?" Erin said, picking up the silver chain.

"That's why this has never happened to Given before—because of the necklace."

Everyone but Given was staring at me with dubious expressions, like the fever had rattled my brain in some way.

"I saw it when you pulled me into the washroom. It was blinking white around the grooves at the bottom, and I remembered being given one after my memory was taken. I remember running through the woods with Given and my necklace getting caught on something inside this old house. It's the only explanation; it has to be."

"Wait," Erin said, putting his hand up. "Your memory was taken?"

"Yes."

"How much do you remember now?" Erin asked, bizarrely pulled away from the gravity of what I was trying to convey.

"That's about it. I'll give you more details later, but I think I lost my necklace by the swamp where you found me."

Erin seemed to be pulled into the present by my words and shook the bewildered look off his face. He looked down at the map. "We might be leaving."

"I think I'll be able to find it when I'm there," I said.

"When you're there?" Erin said, sounding confused.

Madam's expression was severe. "You want to go find it?"

"Yes. I have to."

"No," Erin said.

"I think this necklace is protecting us somehow—from them, from the men in the pinstriped suits."

"We can't speculate anything," Erin said.

"I'm not speculating. I know," I said, holding up my glowing arm for emphasis.

"We know you're still...glowing," Erin said, fumbling awkwardly. "We're going to make a run to the outpost to get supplies and then decide what to do next."

I backpedaled toward the sitting room.

"There might be answers there at the swamp," I said.

"Basil," Erin said, waving me to come back.

I kept stepping backward, and halfway across the room, I could feel my arm beginning to burn again. As soon as I made it across the room, I keeled over, wrapping my arms around my stomach.

"Basil!" Erin called out, rushing over to me.

"It's starting." I wheezed. "I can feel my arm starting to burn. I can feel it in my stomach, too."

"Basil, don't..." Erin's voice evaporated as he looked at the rectangular prism he still clutched in his hand. It was blinking white.

Thirty-Two

"Okay, if we're going to the swamp, you're going to need these," Erin said, handing Given and me each a handkerchief.

Erin marched around the garage, throwing supplies into the Bronco. He wasn't happy. Given and I were in clean clothes, standing side by side and watching Erin storm around the room. I had never seen him look so mad before.

"I wish there was another way. I don't like this plan," Erin muttered. He turned to both of us. "This has the potential to be very dangerous." He stalked over to the trunk, inspecting the small bag he'd packed, probably stalling to see if either of us was going to back out.

"Are you sure?" Given asked me.

"What if there are answers for us?" I said.

"That's all I can think about, too," Given said, opening up the passenger's side door for me. "But what if there's only a necklace there, or what if there's nothing?"

"There are answers there. I know it," I said, wishing I felt more confident about my decision.

"Here," Given said as he placed his necklace over my head and around my neck. "To keep you safe."

"You should have it," I said, starting to take it off.

"No," Given said, pushing my hands down.

"It's your necklace."

"I want you to wear it, okay?" Given said. His voice held a weight of finality, forcing me not to press the issue.

"Okay, but don't get any farther than twenty feet away," I said. "You start to feel the burn after that."

"Feel the burn. Love the burn," Given joked, doing a couple of standing pushups on the Bronco door.

"Given," I said, more serious than I would have liked. "Stay close, okay?"

He winked. "Oh, I'll stay close."

I rolled my eyes at him and climbed into the Bronco.

*

The chilly morning air filled Betsy's cab with a woodsy cinder smell. I had stuck my hand out of the open passenger window, and my fingers drifted on the rapid breeze. I looked down at the black handkerchief Erin had handed me. As we got closer to the swamp, the road was less defined, and it twisted closer between the trees. The cab suddenly filled with a repulsive, sewage smell. I quickly placed the handkerchief over my nose and mouth, which stifled a lot of the stench.

"Almost there," Erin said, pulling up his handkerchief.

I looked over at Given as we bounced around in our seats from the roughness of the road. I tied my handkerchief around my face and rolled up the window. The thin glass didn't protect us from the reeking scent of rotting waste, the type of smell that pushed away civilization.

"We're here," Erin said, putting Betsy in park.

We filed out of Betsy. The forest looked like the one that consumed the Manor, a slow and savage takeover from years of neglect.

"Where's the swamp?" I asked.

Erin pointed at a wall of untamed bushes, a mess of ivy, shrubs, and broken tree branches. Given and I traveled toward it while Erin hesitated by the Bronco. We pushed past the wall of green, clawing at the foliage that blocked our way. As we broke past the wall, this greenish-brown pond came into view. I suddenly realized that whoever had named this sewage pit The Swamp was being overly generous. There were dozens of objects floating on top of the thick, contaminated water, from branches and dried leaves to metal barrels and broken mattresses. This swamp looked secluded, untouched, making me think of the day Erin and Madam had found me. I turned around and saw Erin staring at the two of us with his back pushed up against the bush wall.

"We found you at the edge of the swamp," Erin said, pointing with his finger. "Kind of by that tree."

I turned back around and trekked to the base of a tree. It was so decayed that I wasn't sure anyone could tell type of tree it was. I could see the tip of a house off in the distance.

"Does any of this look familiar to you guys?" Erin asked.

"Sort of," Given said, running his hand through his hair.

I journeyed around the edge of the swamp and headed for the house, peeking over my shoulder to make sure Given was following me. Until we found my necklace, we were chained together, in a sense.

"Basil, wait," Erin called after me, but I pressed forward.

The forest was more ravaged than the one I was used to trekking through, but the pull of finding out more information about my past kept me moving. We climbed over fallen tree trunks and forced our way through more wildly growing ivy and barbarian bushes, until we came face to face with an ancient house that looked somewhat familiar. The cement stairs were cracked and caked in weeds, but I climbed them to the front door anyway. When I turned the knob, the door opened with a loud screech. Erin and Given peeked over my shoulders, looking inside the decrepit house decayed from neglect. Ivy covered the windows, blocking most of the light, and an odd, cool breeze brushed past my cheeks. I took a step forward, but Erin's hand gripped my arm and pulled me back.

"I'll go first," Erin said in his firm voice.

The floorboards, covered in vines and underbrush, groaned with Erin's added weight. When he reached the center of the living room, Erin waved us in.

"Just be careful where you walk. These floorboards don't look too sturdy," Erin said, examining the wood underneath his sneakers.

Given slipped in front of me and proceeded to voyage into the house. After a few steps, he turned and held out his hand for me, whispering, "Fair Maiden."

I glanced at his inviting palm and then up into his silver eyes. They were gentle and indulging. I slid my hand into his; with my touch, he gave me a wink. I chuckled softly, rolling my eyes at him. As Given laced his fingers with mine, my hand sizzled and my cheeks flushed.

As I stepped inside the house, we both turned our attention back to the problem at hand—finding my necklace. We walked slowly, cautiously together, our fingers still entwined. As I rounded the corner of the little foyer, there was an enormous tree growing out of the floorboards and into the walls of the house. The branches crawled along the walls, lining the tea-shaded paint with dead leaves. I hadn't realized I'd stopped moving until Given gave my hand a light squeeze.

"That looks familiar," I breathed, pointing at the tree planted in the other room.

I walked more quickly toward the tree, practically dragging Given with me. Erin was standing in the middle of a closet doorframe close by. I slipped inside the room the tree had grown into. Part of its roots twisted up, making the floor splinter. The room looked like a sunroom. From the ceiling to the walls, dusty, cracked windows were everywhere. Dingy, ripped chairs and a broken table rested inside the room, set up symmetrically. I ran my fingers along the bark of the old tree, feeling an old memory tug at my brain.

"I think I remember this room," Given said, swiping two of his fingers along the dusty glass, leaving two clean trails behind.

I examined the tree more closely, and a flicker of light caught my eye. I dropped down on my knees and peered into the roots.

"I found it," I said triumphantly, watching the necklace shimmer up at me happily.

I grabbed at it, but it was entangled with roots and vines.

"You got it?" Given asked, kneeling down next to me.

I pulled at it harder.

"Let me try," Given said, moving his hands toward mine. He shifted some roots and vines. "Got it."

He pulled the necklace out and held it up. It had dulled in the time since it had been abandoned. The silver winked at me in a lackluster sort of way as Given placed it around his neck.

"You have mine, and I have yours," he said with his half-cocked smile pinned to his face.

"Okay, let's go," Erin said, popping into the room.

"We should search the house," I said.

"Yeah, see if there is any information here," Given agreed.

Erin paused for a moment and finally gave in. "Just for a little bit."

We were leaving the sunroom, when we heard the floorboards moan from another room. We froze dead in our tracks, listening intently, trying to hear what had made the noise. There was another moan followed by a harsh, mechanical growl. It was soft and low, but we all knew what it was.

I looked around to see if there was a way out when I saw the staircase, a winding iron one that twisted through an opening in the ceiling, leading to the next floor. I tapped Given and pointed to it. Given did the same to Erin, who took another survey of our surroundings and then nodded his head.

Slowly, he mouthed.

More carefully, slower than before, we worked our way to the stairs. I was the first on the stairs, followed closely by Given. Erin was a step away from the stairs when the floor below him moaned. We froze. Our breaths waited inside our lungs, afraid to escape. I looked around to see the wolf-like machine stalking across the floor. When Erin took another step, the wolf bolted for us.

"Run!" Erin yelled.

The sound of our feet hitting the iron staircase filled my ears. The second floor was even more broken down than the first, moaning with every move we made. Growls and the sounds of metal clanking against iron filled my ears. I opened doors frantically down the long hallway, trying to find a way out, finding only closets and enclosed washrooms. Given opened a door, and Erin pushed me through the threshold. Erin closed the door with so much force the walls shook.

There was a loud bang against the door as the wolf tried to break in. Erin fell onto the floor; his ripped pant leg was bright with crimson. Given's face shifted as he ran to Erin and examined his wound.

"I'm fine," Erin said through clenched teeth. "Just a scratch."

Given took his handkerchief from his neck and tied it around Erin's calf. I looked around the room to see if there was a way out. It was a plain room with dingy yellow sheets, a few pillows, and a couple of other random items. A sliding glass door led out to a balcony, but the glass was broken and leaves blew into the room. I could see the Bronco from here. It was so painfully close.

"Anything?" Given asked.

"The balcony doesn't look very stable," I said.

"Look! A crawlspace," Erin said, pointing to the ceiling.

"I think that's our only option," Given said, getting up and tossing a stack of books from an old, rickety-looking chair. Given climbed on top of the chair and opened the panel to the crawlspace. He glared at me. "You first."

"No," I said, shaking my head. "You need to go first so you can pull up Erin."

The banging turned into scratching, and the sound of wood splintering bounced around us. Another bang rang out with more wood being ripped away. It was getting closer.

"Fine," Given huffed, knowing there was no time to argue.

He pulled himself into the crawlspace, and I helped Erin to his feet and up onto the chair. Given grabbed Erin's hand and heaved him up. More wood cracked and fractured as metal claws hacked away at it. As I reached for Given's hand, the wolf broke through the door.

It charged for me, hitting the chair I was standing on. I quickly grabbed Given's hand, but I didn't have a good enough grip, and I slipped from his fingers. I scrambled to my feet, as the wolf turned around, staring straight at me. It began to circle around me, and for some strange reason, I wondered if it was the same one from Gina's. I looked up at Given, who held out his arm as far as he could so I could grab it.

As I took a step forward, the wolf charged, colliding into me with so much force that I crashed through what little remained of the glass door and smacked my hip on the balcony railing. The metal squealed as the railing gave way under our weight. I tumbled forward onto a patch of ivy, and the wolf stumbled a few yards further.

I scrambled to my hands and knees, but the sound of glass cracking stopped me. I wasn't only on a bed of ivy... I was on top of the sunroom. I pushed aside some of the ivy, and sure enough, I saw the couches and chairs inside. I tried to scoot toward the broken balcony, but the glass cracked under my hands.

The wolf stood up and paced back and forth at the edge of the glass. It stepped toward me. More cracks flared out from under its metallic paw.

"No!" Given shouted from the balcony. It was a desperate, panicked scream. "Hey! Over here!" Given yelled, more composed, waving his arms. "Over here! I'm much tastier!"

The wolf glowered back and forth between the two of us but then continued toward me. The glass hissed under its weight.

"No!" Given yelled again.

HISS!

The wolf got closer.

CRACK!

I slid on my stomach, trying to get to a sturdy part of the roof.

SNAP!

The glass gave way, and I began to fall. I grabbed at air and ivy, but everything fell with me. I landed on the couch, which broke under me. Shattered glass fell off my tattered sweater and out of my messy hair as I sat up and scuttled backward on my hands and heels. The wolf rested next to the broken couch, not moving. My head spun, and cold seeped in through the rips in my sweater.

All of a sudden, a hand shot through one of the large cracks in the sunroom windows, gripping me by the shoulder of my sweater, and yanked me through the window, making it shatter in places I didn't fit. I dropped down to the muddy ground as glass rained over me. The first thing I saw was a pair of polished black shoes splattered with mud. I blinked up and saw a brutish man staring down at me, wearing a black pinstriped suit. My heart caught in my throat.

He gripped me with a rough arm around my torso, pinning my arms to my chest. I struggled against his grip, as he pulled me around the house. I managed to wriggle out of his grip, knocking into the wood siding. The blond-haired, broad-shouldered man looked strangely familiar.

"Who are you?" I blurted out, not knowing where the bravado came from.

"I'm sorry, but I don't have a choice," he said, his eyes distraught and troubled.

The man lunged for me, gripping one of my arms and yanking me toward the forest. I dug my heels into the dirt, trying to pull away.

"Erin! Given!" I yelled, twisting my arm in his hand.

He snatched up my ankle, and I fell onto my back, thudding hard against the dirt as he dragged me toward the forest.

"What do you want from me?" I screamed, grabbing at foliage and twigs. "Help!" I grasped a sturdy tree branch.

"Let go," the man grunted, trying to yank me off. He dug into his pocket and pulled out a small flashlight.

"No!" I yelled. But I did let go, and the man toppled backward, losing his grip on me. I scurried over to the flashlight. He yanked it away, and it fell from his hands and tumbled down the steep hill, disappearing into the dense forest.

"Who are you?" I barked, my voice fiercer than I ever thought possible.

"You don't remember me?" he asked, looking confused.

"No. Should I?"

"It was a long time ago," he said, taking a hesitant step forward.

I took a step back, watching his movements closely. I backed up, trying to put more distance between us. When the man made a quick and sudden lunge for me, I turned and ran back in the direction of the house.

"Given! Erin!" I screamed, ducking under branches.

All of a sudden, my legs were pinned, and I fell to the ground once again.

"Basil!" Given's shouted.

"No!" Erin yelled.

Given ran for the man and tried to yank him off me, but he pushed Given away, knocking him into a tree.

"No! You don't understand!" the man shouted desperately.

"Let go," Given grunted, marching over and giving him another yank.

"I can't! This is my only option!"

"Get away from my daughter!" Erin yelled.

Something about that sentence made the man drop his grip on me. Given jerked the man away and pinned him onto the ground. Erin's breaths were staggered as he hobbled over to us. Given let the man go as Erin took a spot between him and me.

"Joe?" Erin's voice was a whisper.

"I can't...ca— I—" Joe stuttered in defeated sobs, "I...this isn't..."

"Joe, you're one of them?" Erin asked, gripping him and giving him a little shake. "How did you find her?"

Joe cupped his face in his hands, shaking his head back and forth. When he pulled his hands away, his face was composed, but his eyes were glassy and ringed in red.

"It's the cuffs," Joe said, reaching for my arm.

"No," Erin said, flinging out his arm to shield me.

Joe pulled back his hand. "I deserve that." He took a breath and rolled up his sleeve, exposing his own etched arm. "They call it a cuff. They are able to track you with it." He took another deep, stuttering breath. "They are called extraction agents, the men in the pinstriped suits."

"What did they do to us?" Given chimed in.

"You," Joe said, pointing at Given. "You're that little boy."

"How do you know us?" I asked.

"You really don't remember me?"

I studied his familiar features, his broad shoulders and course face.

"You were there when I first met Janie," I said, recalling the fuzzy memory.

"Yes," Joe said.

"How did you find her?" Erin asked.

"Through Oddy."

"What? Where is she?" I demanded.

"I don't know."

"How can you not know? You're one of them!" I said.

"I'm just a gofer, a footman. There is a lot I don't know." He took a deep breath, rubbing his eyes with hands. His face was covered in conflict. "I'm sorry, Erin, but they took my Kimmie. They took my little girl, Erin."

It was quiet for a long time. The midday sun peeked through the trees above us.

"What do you mean you found her through Oddy?" Erin asked.

"I don't know the details. I just have a clip from Oddy's memories of Basil and th—"

"You took her memories!" I shouted.

"Keep going, Joe," Erin said, putting his hand on my shoulder.

I took a deep breath, trying to hold myself together.

"That's why the copy drone came after you at Oddy's house. They were waiting for you."

"Copy drone?" Erin asked.

"That wolf machine. It's able to copy, so to speak, pieces of memories. They're after you, Basil. They're closing in on you. You need to leave. For some reason, they're having trouble picking up the Manor—some kind of interference."

"Did you tell them where it is?" Erin asked.

"No! No." Joe shook his head vigorously.

"How do we know you're telling us the truth?"

"I was going to—" Joe's voice lowered as he dropped his eyes to the ground. "—use her as a bartering chip for my daughter. I was starting here and working my way back."

"Aren't you lucky you foun—" Given started to say but cut himself off.

"What?" Joe said.

"Sorry, it's nothing," Given murmured, running his hand through his hair roughly.

Silence lingered in the air. Given stood over Joe, jaw clenched tight, making his veins protrude menacingly as he watched the man cautiously.

"You need to take your girl and get away," Joe told Erin. "They're going to find her if you don't. They find everyone they're looking for."

"Why are they looking for her?" Erin asked.

"I don't know, but you need to go."

Erin struggled to stand on his feet, wincing slightly. "Let's go."

"He could be lying?" asked Given.

"He's not. Given, Basil, we are leaving."

"What if he knows more?" I said, getting to my feet.

"He doesn't." Erin turned to Joe. "I really hope you get your little Kimmie back, but I hope you think long and hard about what you tell them about my girl."

Joe bent his head toward the dirt. "I won't say anything, Erin. Promise."

"Let's go," Erin said, marching away.

Thirty-Three

After Given patched Erin up, we loaded him into Betsy. Given drove us back, clutching the steering wheel so hard that his knuckles were a bright white.

"We shouldn't be leaving him," Given said, his voice full of anger and concern.

"What should we have done, Given? Tie him up? Keep him captive?" Erin asked lightheartedly.

"I don't know," Given said. "It's just... Kids aren't bargaining chips. Going after Basil? He shouldn't have—" His voice faded into angry grumbling. It made me think that Given could relate from one of his many experiences.

"I know Joe," said Erin. We used to be friends. He's just a desperate father. All in all, he's going to have to live with what he's done and what he will do. He won't say anything."

My mind drifted away from the cab of this car, thinking about Oddy and Joe. I pressed my head against the window and closed my eyes.

*

I was in a room with my ear pushed up against a cedar door. I had just met Janie, and then two men had barged their way into the manor. Erin had quickly pushed me into this room.

"There's two of them!" Joe shouted. "Two kids?"

"I found him wandering on the road. What was I supposed to do, Joe?" Janie argued back, the tension in the room infecting her as well.

"Let him keep wandering," Joe hissed.

"Calm down, Joe," Erin said.

"Calm down?" Joe hissed. "Look around, Erin. Everyone is gone. I have my Kimmie to think about."

"I know you do," Erin said.

"You can't do this!" Joe shouted, halfway to losing it. "Those kids need to go!"

The room fell quiet as a soft set of footsteps padded into the room.

"I'm fine, Maggie. You don't need to fuss over me." Madeline's voice traveled through the crowd, carrying experience and authority. "Mr. Dervin, I—"

"I already know what you're going to say, but you have to think about the other families left in this territory, the ones that want to keep their kids safe. Those two might bring more attention."

"Mr. Dervin, you are a strong-willed man, but you still have a lot to learn. Now, I expect no more rude interruptions while I'm speaking."

"So you're going to agree with your daughter and son-in-law?" Joe scoffed.

Madeline cleared her throat harshly. "On the contrary, I don't think it is—how should I say—in the best interest of my grandson for these children to stay."

"What are you talking about, Madeline? Simon has already been taken."

"It's Ms. Wardell to you, Mr. Dervin, and that is precisely what I am talking about." Madeline paced slowly back and forth, and the wood creaked as she did. "My grandson is out there somewhere. He was taken, and if he should get away, I know he will head back home to us. Now, that can't happen if we are all taken for helping these children. So, Mr. Dervin, that is why I agree with you. Those children need to go."

"But Mother, they're only kids," Madam said.

"No." Madeline's voice was harsh. "They are not our problems to worry about. Do you really want to risk any chance of seeing Simon again?"

The room grew quiet with Madeline's harsh but true statement.

"There has to be another way," Erin said.

"I wish there was, Erin, but these children have already worn out their welcome," Madeline said. "Joe, put them on the next available train."

"You can't do this," Janie said, her voice echoing down the hallway.

Heavy soles stomped up to the door, and I backed away, running into the bed as I did. The door flew open, flooding the dark bedroom with light. A hand slipped inside mine. Looking to my side, I saw the little boy with silver eyes. Joe stomped up to us and grabbed us by our hands; he pulled us out of the room, down the hall, and toward the front door.

"Let us figure this out," Erin said, standing in front of the door.

"No," Madeline said bluntly. "It's better this way." She opened the door. "Be on your way, Joe. Maybe you should go with him, George."

"I don't—" George started.

"You will take these kids, and that is final," Madeline stated.

"Come on, George," said Joe.

"Ummm…okay," George said hesitantly as he strolled over to me and grabbed my hand.

George followed Joe and the little boy to a blue car that said Cavalier on its trunk. He set me in the back and buckled my seatbelt. Madam clutched Erin's hand tightly, staring straight at me. I could almost see longing in her eyes, as if she wanted to keep me. If that were true, then why was she letting me go? I still didn't fully understand what was happening.

The rain beat hard against the window as I picked at a thread that had sprung out from the back of the passenger's seat. My mind felt mushy, and my fingers were cold. It felt like I had been sitting forever when Joe pulled his car into park. George opened my door and helped me out of the car, then followed Joe down a dirt path to a dilapidated building.

We pushed through the door into a room crowded with people. All the talking in the room was hushed away. The people stared at the little boy and me as we passed them. Everyone backed away from us, as if we carried a deadly disease.

Joe approached a woman with long, black hair. "Two tickets, please," he said.

The woman stared at me with wide, astonished eyes.

"It's true?" she whispered.

"Lin?" Joe said. "Hello, George's wife?"

"Lin, sweetie," George said, pressing his hand on her arm.

"Oh, right, two tickets," Lin pulled out two tickets from her drawer.

A loud, high-pitched whistle filled the room.

"Attention, all passengers," Lin shouted, getting to her feet. "Please collect all your luggage and follow me out to the loading platform."

Everyone started gathering their things and following Lin out of the building. As we rounded the corner, a large train came into view. Lin was helping people up the ramp and into the train.

"Up you go," George said as he set me on the large, wooden ramp.

"Go and sit," Joe said to the little boy.

I bit my lip, unsure of what to do. The little boy gripped my hand and tugged me up the ramp. We padded inside the train; it was large and dimly lit with worn leather seats. People eyed us warily, as we past them. We traveled down several compartments until we reached one with very few people. When we sat down, the couple who was sitting in the seats facing ours got up and walked away.

Another whistle shouted out from the train, and we began to move, and I looked out the window as Joe and George shrank out of sight. When I couldn't see them anymore, I pressed my forehead to the window and fell asleep.

*

A mechanical growl woke me, and I stared at this massive, wolf-like machine. The machine was hovering over the little boy, whose eyes were glazed over. I pushed the machine off him, making the thing growl again. I shook the little boy, trying to wake him from his daydreaming stupor. He shook his head, and I pulled him to his feet, then pushed him out of the row

227

and down the walkway. The machine jumped on me, knocking us both to the ground. The boy looked confused and dazed. The machine flipped me over, and I felt this pulling inside my brain as two green lights like great, glowing eyes stared down at me. My brain felt like it was spinning inside my skull. My heart ran rapidly inside my chest.

The wolf was suddenly kicked away, skidding along the metal floor, filling the train cart with a loud screech. Everything was still spinning. The wolf quickly rose on its legs, poised and ready. The car rocked as the train stopped. A whistle filled the air around us as the boy suddenly pulled me to my feet. The wolf darted for us, and we ran down the walkway and into the next car and then the next.

We heard the clack of metal against metal as the machine broke its way into each car. As the boy opened yet another door, large crates and barrels blocked our way, but we climbed up and over them, hoping it would lead us out.

"Hey, kids!" someone shouted out to us from the direction we were headed. "It's me, Erin."

The man from that enormous house!

My head was still spinning, and my energy was running out. Erin squeezed through the crates and barrels to reach us. He scooped us up and pulled us toward a door. As we stepped through the door, the crisp night air surrounded me. I peeked back, trying to see where the wolf had gone, but I couldn't find it. Erin carried us to his large car. He plopped us inside and buckled us up, and we drove far away from the train, far away from the wolf. Betsy skidded to a stop when an SUV came into view, and Erin jumped out of the Bronco.

"Made it just in time," Erin said.

"Bring them out," said Madeline.

Erin pulled us out, leaving us to stand by the Bronco's large tire on the passenger's side. I pressed my hand to my forehead; my brain felt like mush sloshing around inside my skull.

"I almost believed you, Madeline," Erin said.

"I did believe you," said Janie.

"It's okay, Janie," Madam replied. "my mom can be very convincing."

"Too many people knew," Madeline explained. "It had only been a few days, and the whole territory was talking about them."

"You need to take him and go, Janie." Erin scooped up the little boy and placed him in the SUV.

"I'll keep him safe," she said, opening the driver's side door.

"We know you will," said Madam.

"We'll figure something out for the girl," Erin added. "Just go."

Janie drove away, and the little boy with the silver eyes waved goodbye. Erin scooped me up and put me back inside his car, and once Madam and Madeline had both climbed in, we drove away. The gentle rocking of the car lulled me further into my stupor. I fell asleep, not quite sure what was real anymore.

Thirty-Four

I was awoken by someone shaking my arm. Given's silver eyes greeted me; he was clutching my door open with one hand. Betsy's dome light was bright in the dim garage.

Given smiled a sad smile. "Hey."

I smiled back. "Hi."

"We're home."

I unbuckled my seatbelt and slid out of the Bronco. The backseat was empty when I glanced back to see Erin.

"I already helped Erin into the manor. He's talking with Bobby and Madam, telling them what happened and everything."

"Hey, Given?"

"Yeah?"

"Are you okay?"

"Yes. I should be asking you that," he said, lightly touching the arm of my sweater. It was battered and ripped from my encounters with the wolf and Joe.

"I'm fine," I said, clutching my hands together. I took a hesitant breath. "Given?"

"Yes?"

"Do you remember Joe?"

"Barely. But my mom says I was kind of out of it for the first couple of days."

"Really?"

"I think it was because of what they did to us, the whole memory wipe thing," he said, opening up the garage door for me.

"That makes sense."

We entered the foyer, and as we passed the stairs, I kicked off my shoes and placed them underneath the small hall table. I was trying to do it before Madam saw the mud caked all over them.

I pointed at Given's boots. "You might—"

"Oh my goodness!" Madam exclaimed. "You two look terrible."

We went into the sitting room, and Madam and Bobby stood in front of Erin. Janie was crouched next to Erin's leg. I looked down at myself and then over at Given to find us covered with scratches and mud.

"Are you both okay?" Madam asked.

"It looks worse than it is," Given said with a shrug of his shoulders.

"Basil?" Madam asked.

"I'm fine, really."

"Oh." Madam looked us up and down. "Okay. Well, you two should get cleaned up then." Madam's eyes looked glazed over, as if her mind were somewhere else.

"Are you okay, Madam?" I asked.

She was suddenly back in the present, narrowing her eyes at me. "I'm fine. Don't fuss over me. Now go get cleaned up." She emphasized her words by nudging us into the foyer and toward the stairs.

*

After cleaning up and changing clothes, I met up with Given by the stairs. His hair was wet, making it look black, and he held a black and green flannel shirt in his hands. I fidgeted with the sweater I was holding. Given gave me a smile, and when he turned to head down the stairs, I saw a bright red cut running from his shoulder and hiding beneath his gray ribbed tee.

"Oh my goodness," I said, grabbing his arm and angling his back toward me.

"You know, all three of you say that phrase." Given chuckled and turned to face me.

"What happened?"

"You, Madam, and Madeline. You all say, 'Oh, my goodness.'" He laughed again. "It's cute."

"Your back," I said, trying to turn him around to get a better look.

"Yeah, I couldn't quite get it," he said, stretching his neck to look at his back.

We headed downstairs into the sitting room. Erin lay across the couch with his hurt leg underneath the bulky surgical machine they called the surgeon. It hummed loudly, and the sound reminded me of the day Given found me in the woods and used the surgeon to fix my broken arm. Janie pushed over the red duffle bag with her foot. We sat on the floor next to the duffle bag, close to Erin and Janie. Given unzipped the duffle bag and pulled out cleansing wipes. I dabbed peroxide down Given's cut, which ran all the way to his spine.

"How did you manage to do this to yourself?" I asked, pushing aside his gray ribbed tee.

"I'm not exactly sure. Maybe when we were running for our lives," Given said inside a snicker, shrugging as he did.

He was calm and collected as always.

"Hold still," I said, pushing down his other shoulder with my hand.

"Now, you sound like me."

"You don't have to insult the poor girl," Janie said from the couch as she pressed buttons on the bulky surgical machine.

I dug through the red medical bag and pulled out a small stack of gauze pads and medical tape. I tried to focus on patching him up, not on Joe or the wolf or anything else.

"Okay," Janie said, pulling on a leaver that released Erin's leg. "All done."

"Thanks, Janie," Erin said, throwing his legs over the couch next to Given and me.

She smiled. "It's what I do."

"Looks like you're done too," I said, positioning the last strip of tape on the gauze pads on Given's back.

"Thank you, Basil," he said, shrugging on his green flannel shirt.

"So what now?" Janie asked, shutting down the machine; Given passed her the thick plastic case the machine went in.

"We leave," Erin said, resting his elbows on his knees, making him look older.

"I know. I guess what I meant was... Can we really trust Joe?"

"Whether we can or not, leaving looks like our safest option right now." Erin frowned down at Given and me. "Maggie and

Bobby are upstairs packing. Why don't you kids go up and help?"

"Okay," Given said, getting up off the ground.

"Where are we going, Erin?" I asked, getting to my feet too.

"Someplace safe," Erin said, rubbing his eyes with his palms. "Now, you'd best get your stuff together. I don't know when we'll be back."

"Okay," I whispered, heading out of the sitting room.

Given followed me as we made our way up the gigantic staircase. I suddenly stopped mid-stride, and Given ran into my back.

"Oh," I said, my voice ringing with a ping of forgetfulness.

"You forget something?" he asked, raising one of his eyebrows.

"A lot of things, apparently." I chuckled softly, as my lips arched into a strange, half smile.

"It's easier to laugh about it, isn't it?" Given smiled softly, holding the inside joke safely between us.

"Better than letting it defeat you," I said with a shrug.

"Now, there's the fair maiden I know. The one that smacked the door in my face when we first met," Given said, smiling down at me.

My cheeks flushed. "Met again."

"Met again-again if you want to be technical," Given said with his half-cocked smile pinned to his face. "So what did you forget this time?"

"My sweater."

"I'll get it."

"No, I got it," I said, gripping his arm and tugging him back. "I'll meet you upstairs."

"I can grab it."

"No, really. It's okay."

"Okay," Given said, passing me.

I went downstairs and headed toward the sitting room.

"Erin, what are you saying?" Janie asked in a hushed whisper.

"You know what I'm saying, Janie. Get your boy and get out of here." Erin's voice held an odd, brash tone.

"We're not splitting up. Besides, I thought you had someplace safe to go to."

Erin chuckled darkly. "A couple of hours ago, I would have considered this place safe, but now? Now I feel like I'm sitting in the middle of one big target sign with the bullseye resting on our front door." He stood up and paced a couple of times before stopping abruptly. "I have this horrible feeling, Janie, that Joe is right. I feel like they're going to break in at any moment and take my little girl away from me."

It was quiet for a while. I held my breath as Erin paced back and forth with weighted steps.

"Erin, you know that's not going to happen," Janie said in a smooth, coaxing voice, but she had paused too long for that sentence to be reassuring.

"Do I? Do you? We don't know anything anymore. All I know is that Given hasn't had any problems, not until recently. Not until he started—" he cut himself off, taking out his anger with his steps on the hardwood floor.

"Not until he started hanging around Basil?" Janie sounded irritated. "Is that where this is going?"

"Janie, don't get defensive," Erin said. "This conversation should be going the other way around, actually."

"What is that supposed to mean, Erin?"

It was quiet for a second or two.

"It means nothing, Janie." Erin took a harsh breath. "Look, you can say no all you want, but ultimately, Given should have a say in his own wellbeing."

"I'll talk to him, okay?"

"Thank you. That's all I ask," Erin said.

Thirty-Five

When Erin and Janie came upstairs, everyone was in my room, and bags were piled on top of my bed. I was in the middle of throwing my clothes into my bag.

"Make sure you bring warm clothes," Madam said, looking inside my bag.

"Given, can I talk to you for a second?" Janie said, waving him over with just her index finger.

"Sure, Mom."

I bit my lip as they disappeared into the hallway.

"I hope this is warm enough," Madam said, swishing one of my cotton t-shirts between her fingertips as she eyed my battered snickers warily. "I think..." Madam started, but she trailed off, as she headed out of my room.

I followed her down the hallway into her bedroom. She didn't shoo me away. Madam headed into their walk-in closet, and I waited outside. Madam was out of the closet within a few minutes, lugging a large cardboard box with her.

"They may be a little big," Madam said, flipping up the flaps of the box, "but I guess it will give you some growing room." There was a hitch in her voice that I didn't quite understand.

"Thank you," I whispered, looking into the box.

"I was waiting until you got a bit older, but..." She pulled out a brown leather jacket and held it out for me. "Try it on and see if it fits."

I slipped my arms into the thick, smooth jacket. The leather was worn from age, making it soft and inviting. It wasn't until I pulled the jacket over my shoulders that I realized Madam had a specific smell, a musky floral scent.

"These are from when I was younger, back when dinosaurs roamed the earth," Madam joked. Reminiscence pulled her lips into a minute smile. It made me wonder about the kind of person she was when she was my age. She pulled out a pair of jeans, a red hooded sweater, and a pair of boots.

I picked up the leather boots, examining them closely. They not only seemed practical, but stylish too, and they matched the jacket as a perfect combo. I looked up at Madam, and her face seemed weirdly soft. She got up and headed back into the closet, pulled out a black sweater, and then went back in for a scarf. As I examined the black sweater, something crinkled inside one of the pockets. I pulled out a piece of paper. Neat, black writing caught my attention first; I noticed the weight of the paper second. It wasn't a note but a picture. I unfolded it with Madam's beautiful script facing me. Simon's ready to be a big brother.

I quickly flipped the picture over, and Madam's beaming face stared back at me. She was laughing as she touched Simon's cheek softly with one hand. Simon had this weird expression on his face, as his hand lay against her stomach. Madam's stomach was plump and round—a mother's belly.

"We should really get go—" Madam's voice faded into nothingness, as she looked at the picture in my hands.

"It was in the black sweater," I whispered quickly.

She marched up to me, quickly snatching the picture out of my hands. Her face hardened within seconds.

"I... I'm s-sorry," I stuttered, nerves making me bite my lip and clasp my hands together.

Madam was quiet as she stared at the picture. She unconsciously dropped the cream-colored scarf as she ran her fingers down the side of the picture. Tears sprouted from the corner of her eyes and rolled down her cheeks. I had never seen Madam cry before now. I suddenly felt very awkward and wanted to leave, but I was unable to move. The room was silent for an uncomfortable amount of time. My eyes traveled everywhere but directly at Madam. I had no idea she had so much emotion stored inside of her. Finally, I built up enough courage to scoop up the things Madam had given me and began making strides for the door.

I was halfway across the room when I heard, "Wait." Madam's voice was softer than I ever remember hearing it. "Basil," she said, taking a step toward me. "I'm sorry."

"Huh?"

"Simon was feeling the baby kick for the first time." She wore a sad but proud smile. "The baby died a couple of days later." Madam took slow, steady strides toward me. "And then, when Simon was taken, I—" Madam gulped, taking an unsteady breath. "I built more walls."

"I'm sorry."

"No," Madam said with a single, soft stroke to my arm. "I'm sorry. I guess I was afraid. I am afraid."

The room was silent again. I stared down at Madam's hand resting on my arm, a comforting gesture. I looked up into Madam's sapphire eyes. They flickered with years of sadness.

"Of what?" I asked. The whole conversation felt bizarre to me, like I had stepped into an alternate reality.

"Of losing you, too." Her eyes were glassy with emotion.

"Oh," I said, feeling like it was a dumb response.

"But Basil," Madam started and then suddenly became fervent and serious. She put her hand on my cheek. "Don't ever doubt that I love you."

My back was stiff. I had no idea what to do, so I just blinked up at her, trying to soak in her words. She took the stack of clothes from my hands and placed them on her desk off to the side, determination never faltering from her face.

"I will try harder. You deserve it." She pulled me into a hug, wrapping her arms around me awkwardly. At first, we were both cold and stiff, but then the ice began to melt, and the hug felt more natural.

"Thank you," I said, pulling her closer.

"I love you, Basil," Madam said, clutching me tighter. "Unconditionally."

Thirty-Six

Madam and I strolled into my bedroom, and everybody was there fiddling with one bag or another. I threw the things Madam had given me into my bag and zipped it up.

"Okay," Given said, standing up. "I'm going to head out."

A jolt surged through my heart.

"You're leaving?" I said, trying to hold in my disappointment, because it was better that way.

"Yeah?" He sounded bemused, as if I should have known this was coming.

"Where are you going?"

Given grabbed my bag and another random bag off my bed. "To the Bronco?"

"Wait, what?"

"Well, I thought about trying to load the cars up using happy thoughts and woodland creatures, but I need some exercise." Given chuckled, adjusting the bags in his hands.

"I mean, after we're done loading everything. Where are you and your Mom headed?"

"The outpost, right?" Given said, eyeing me warily and then turned to Erin. "We're going to the outpost for supplies first, right?"

"Yeah. It's going to be you, me, Bobby, and Basil in the Bronco. Maggie, Madeline, and your mom are going to be following us in the SUV. The SUV goes to get extra gas, and the Bronco is picking up supplies."

"Oh, that's right." Given turned back to me. "You missed our little team meeting."

I grabbed two random bags and followed him through the hallway and down the stairs. We squeezed through the door leading into the garage.

"Why are you coming with us?" I asked, as Given took a bag from my hands and loaded it into the Bronco.

"What do you mean?" he asked, fixing the stack of bags. "We're in this together."

"No," I said, throwing the last bag into the trunk. "I'm leaving because I have to. You—you don't have to."

"Umm, hello." He pulled up his flannel shirt to reveal his etching. "Earth to Basil." He grabbed my arm then and pulled up my sweatband, revealing mine. Lacing his fingers with mine, he lifted our hands up so that our forearms touched, etching against etching. "We're in this together."

My heart sputtered so fast inside my chest that I felt lightheaded. Given's eyes were so enticingly silver; they threatened to lull me into a state of peace I couldn't find anywhere else.

"You don't have to," I said, pulling my hand way from his and shutting the Bronco's trunk.

"I want to, anyway. So why does it matter?"

"Maybe it would be—" I took a gulp of air. "—better if we split ways. You'd be safer." I pulled my sweatband back into position over my etching.

"No, we stick together. Neither of us is safe, Basil."

"No, I'm not safe, Given!" I shouted, smacking my hand against the car, because it was true; because I had to let him go; because he was better off without me. The emotions hit me so hard, it was as if they tackled me from the side.

Given suddenly understood the seriousness of my words, and the humor faded from his face. "Basil." His face was solemn, but his voice was calm.

"You're safe, Given." I pressed my hand against his chest and stared up into his extraterrestrial eyes; I could feel tears building behind mine. "You. Just you. You're safe."

"Basil, I'm not," Given said, laying his hand atop mine. "My etching lit up just like yours. The burning, the headache, the vomiting—everything was the same."

I almost burst into tears right there in front of him, just a puddle of liquid Basil at his feet, because it was all my fault that he'd had to suffer through that. I was leading them straight to him. I knew what was right and wrong here. I knew having Given stay with me just because I wanted him to always be with me was the wrong thing. I knew what I had to do.

"The truth is," I said, taking a breath for courage. "I don't want you to come." It came out in a pathetic whisper, but I somehow managed to push the sentence through my lips.

Given took a step closer, placing his hand on my cheek. "Why are you doing this?"

As much as I wanted to lean into his hand, press my cheek into his palm, I couldn't. I pushed his hand away and took a step back. "You need to leave. I don't want you here," I said, and there was no hesitation that time.

"I don't believe you," Given said, stepping up to me and bending his knees until his eyes met mine. "I'm going, and I'm not changing my mind. What's this really about?"

"I don't want you to come."

"Yes, you told me that. Why?"

"Because."

"Because?" He raised an eyebrow. "Because you think you can protect me? That's what this is about?"

"No. I just don't want you to come."

"You know what, Basil? You can't protect me."

"You need to go." I turned to leave, but Given spun me around and entwined me in his arms.

"Let me go," I said, struggling against his grip.

Given spoke quickly and forcefully, saying each word as if it weighed a thousand pounds on his heart. "I see you, Basil. I see right through this façade. I know you're scared, not just for yourself, but for me. I get that. I get you. You're self-sacrificing that way, but what you don't understand is that I need—" His voice abruptly cut off as the garage door whined open, and his arms dropped from my frame. "You're stuck with me, fair maiden, and that's just the way it is," he said with a half-serious smile.

"Leave. Now," I barked at him.

"Basil. Given. What's going on?" Erin said abruptly.

He walked over to us, as Madam, Janie, Bobby, and Madeline followed him.

"Erin, I don't want him coming. It will be safer if we separate," I said.

"Safer for whom?" Given asked, irritation hardening his voice. "I'm not scared. And you know I'm on that list, too. So don't go on about keeping me safe."

"For me!" I yelled. "It will be safer for me!"

"Yeah, right," he scoffed.

"Well—" Erin started.

"No!" Given interrupted, looking fiercer than I'd ever seen him look. "Don't listen to her! She's just saying that because she knows you want to keep her safe."

"We make a bigger target," I said, trying desperately to get Erin on my side.

"Stop this, Basil," Given demanded, clutching my arm.

"Together, we'll just pull each other down."

"Stop," he said as he turned me in front of him and rested his hands on my shoulders. "Stop making me fight you, Basil."

"No," I began again, pulling away from his hands, "I think w—"

"Oh my goodness!" Madeline shouted, and everyone stared at her as she began to laugh.

She was laughing? I was trying my hardest to protect Given, and she was laughing?

"I don't see how this is funny," Given said, in a harsh, matter-of-fact way.

"Oh, calm down, child." Madeline laughed some more. "The young are so dramatic."

Erin started to chuckle, and Bobby and Janie joined in as well as Madam's lips squished into an awkward half-smile. Given and I glared at each other, our cheeks still hot with anger.

"Well, pish posh to it all. Let's get this show on the road," Madeline said.

"What?" I asked.

"You think too much, child," she replied as she moseyed up to me and patted my cheek.

"Huh?" Given looked as confused as I was.

The laughter died down, and Madeline hobbled to the SUV door. Given took a step toward me, his face covered in frustration and words he couldn't say.

"Never mind," he muttered to himself and headed out of the garage.

As the door closed behind him, everyone went for the trunks and started loading up the two cars as if nothing had even happened. Madeline was having difficulty getting up into the SUV, so I gripped her arm and helped her into the passenger's seat.

"The boy is crazy. I can see it," Madeline said, not letting go of my arm. "And Erin is a crazy boy, too. Just as Maggie can't stop Erin from being Erin, you're not going to stop Given from being Given either. So let's get going, shall we?"

Thirty-Seven

The sign for The Outpost came into view first; the black spray paint was old and faded. The broken-down high school quickly came next. Janie waved at us before we parted ways, and they headed toward the crumbling football stadium. We followed the train tracks up to the makeshift train station, which was actually a couple of hollowed out classrooms with a broken desk.

"Hey, George!" Erin yelled toward the open door.

"Hey!" George shouted, waving at us as we piled out of Betsy.

George was a fair-skinned, petite man, with almond-shaped eyes, and receding, jet-black hair. "You're early," he said.

"We just need to get some supplies from the shop. Can you help us out?" Erin asked.

"Sure. Sure. Next train doesn't come for another hour." He went back into the station and came out with a set of keys.

"Thanks," Erin said.

"Hey, I haven't seen all of you together before," George said, taking us all in. "Just you four?"

"No, Maggs is over getting gas with Janie and Madeline."

"Oh, okay. So they're with my wife," George said, unlocking the small market that used to be a library. The doors whined loudly as he opened them.

"What's going on, Erin?" George said, looking more serious now that the library doors were closed.

"We're kind of taking a vacation," Erin said. "Why don't you guys get some of the supplies we talked about, hmm?" Erin suggested, widening his eyes at us.

"We should split up to save time," Bobby said, drifting off in one direction.

I turned around, and Given was staring right at me. We hadn't talked at all on the way here. I'd sat up front with Erin, and he'd sat in the back with Bobby. Frankly, I didn't know where we stood.

"I agree," I said, heading in the opposite direction of Bobby.

I searched through the canned goods section, grabbing as much as I could carry. I was about to round the corner, when I spotted a can of corn and remembered that Erin loved corn.

"Hurry up, okay?" Erin shouted as the squeak of the library doors bounced off the walls.

I stared at the corn, wondering if it was worth possibly dropping my armload for one tiny can. I decided to try to juggle it all, but just as I reached out to grip the can, a hand covered my mouth. Fear pumped cold shock into my chest. I spun around, and Given's face came into view. He pressed his index finger to his lips, telling me to keep quiet.

"What's going on?" I whispered.

"Shh," he said, pulling me down to the floor and began taking the cans out of my hands. He put them on the floor, up against the wall and grabbed my hand. We crawled through the shelves together as quietly as possible.

"Like I told you, sir," George said, "I haven't seen a kid in over a decade."

"What about you?" a man with a smooth voice asked. "Who were you talking to?"

"He was talking to me," Bobby said.

I peeked around the corner and felt my heart leap up into my throat. A man in a pinstriped suit was standing with George, Erin, and Bobby. Time seemed to stop for a minute or two, and air couldn't escape my lungs.

"Have you seen this girl?" the man in the pinstriped suit asked as he displayed a three-dimensional image of me.

I clutched Given's hand for support, and he squeezed.

"We think she is with a companion, a boy." The man pressed buttons on a sleek metallic pad. Another image appeared, and it was Given as a little boy. "He may look something like this now." The man pressed a few more buttons, and the boy began to age, stopping as a young man that resembled Given almost exactly.

We glanced at each other, took one last look at the group, and headed for the back exit. As we pushed open the door, bushes blocked our way, so we had to squeeze through and crawl along the shrubbery.

"Let's head to the SUV and get them out," Given said.

"What about Erin and Bobby?"

He shook his head. "I don't know."

We ran for the next set of classrooms and climbed through a broken window. We pushed past branches and underbrush.

Squeezing through the doors, we snaked through the room after room, only stopping when we heard a branch break off in the distance. We moved in the opposite direction from where we'd heard the noise and crouched down below a window as a man in a pinstriped suit marched past it. When he was gone, we crept into an office through a large window. A piece of glass broke off and shattered against the ground, filling the quietness with a loud crash.

All I heard then was pounding soles on cold cement. Given pulled me into another office, closing the door behind himself, and we ran through bushes and broken office desks. A door burst open somewhere behind us, and the sound of wood breaking chased us. We moved faster, practically falling out of the next window. Inside a restroom, Given pushed open a stall door and jumped on top of the toilet. He covered his hand with his sweater and broke open the window. Glass fell down as he cleared it from the edges, and he reached for me, helping me up and through the window. I dropped down into a patch of half-living rosebushes. Thorns bit and scratched me as I descended onto them. Given quickly came next.

The men were breaking past the stall doors inside the restroom, and we frantically pushed through the rosebushes. As soon as we'd made it through, we ran into a large building that looked like it had once been a health clinic. We ran past broken surgical equipment and monitors that lay off to the side, rusting and collecting dust. Given pushed aside a door that had broken off its hinges, and we ran back outside.

We crept down the side of the health clinic and peeked around the corner, where I saw a man in a pinstriped suit. I turned to Given, shaking my head. We slunk down the other way. Given looked around the corner and quickly pulled back.

A crash sounded from somewhere inside the health clinic. They would surely find us if we stayed here much longer. I stared at the tall stone wall that trapped us in this little alley, wishing there was some secret passage.

Given waved me over. "We'll have a better chance if we split up. I'll head back to Erin and Bobby. You head to Madam and my Mom."

"Okay," I whispered, pulling away.

"Basil. Wait." His voice was sweet but also sad as he pressed his cheek against mine.

"Be safe," I whispered, closing my eyes as I took a deep breath of soap and aloe.

"I never told you this, but you smell like catcher season—rain and cinder. I love the smell of catcher season." Given took a deep breath, as if he were trying to soak in this moment. "Don't forget me, okay?" His voice was gentle, humming like a lullaby as it drifted past my ear. "Don't forget me. Please."

"We'll make it through this," I whispered, trying to be bold and brave, everything I wasn't.

"Basil?"

"Yeah?"

"Run fast, okay? Get my mom out of here. Get Madam and Madeline to safety." Given kissed my cheek, and we ran in opposite directions.

I was running towards the other end of health clinic when I heard a sudden clinking sound. I looked down and realized that I was wearing both of the rectangular prisms—mine and Given's. I stopped abruptly and turned around. Given was at the end of the alley. His etching beamed a bright yellow-gold. My heart caught in my throat as Given glanced back at me. I shook my head and started to stride toward him.

Run, he mouthed and then disappeared around the corner.

"This way!" one of the men yelled.

A sudden jolt through my heart made me stop mid-stride and clutch my chest. I took a deep, staggered breath, trying to stay sane, trying to keep from screaming. I turned around in shock and disbelief, staring down the calm, empty path. I took a calmer breath and ran toward the crumbling stadium. I ran as fast as I could, trying to push down the fact that I left Given behind, the fact that that crazy boy had given himself up for me.

Thirty-Eight

As I ran into the stadium, Janie and Madam saw me first. Madeline was still sitting in the front seat of the SUV, and Janie and Madam were putting jugs of gas into the trunk.

"Basil?" Madam's expression was one of bewilderment.

"We have to go," I said, closing the trunk door.

"What's going on?" Janie asked.

"We have to leave now. They're here. We have to go now," I repeated, tugging Madam to the passenger's seat and Janie to the driver's seat.

"What about Erin, Bobby, and Given?" Janie asked.

I had to get them to safety. It was the last thing I'd promised Given, and I was going to keep it.

"They have the Bronco," I said, opening their doors and nudging them inside. It wasn't technically a lie, because they could still use the Bronco if they could get to it.

"Okay," Janie said slowly, unease fluttering around her agreement.

We piled into the SUV and started driving down the road. The rocky terrain shook the vehicle, making my necklaces clank against one another.

Madam looked at the prisms and then up at me. "Given's not in the Bronco, is he?" she asked.

I was suddenly pelted with a lurching in my heart. It was so strong that tears instantly sprang from my eyes and trailed down my cheeks. A sob rose up my throat, and I couldn't hold it in. My heart was fracturing, as if the men in the pinstriped suits had taken chunks of it with them when they'd stolen Given from me. More tears and more sobs clogged my throat. My entire body shuddered.

"He used himself as a distraction, didn't he?" Madam asked.

I nodded.

"I… I" my voice quivered as I tried to push it out of my mouth. "I should've s-st-stopped him."

I dropped my face into the cushions of the SUV, which was a mistake, because they smelled like Given. The smell was such a precise replica that if I closed my eyes, I could pretend he was still with me.

"I should've done something!" I cried into the cushion. "Anything."

I looked over at Janie, whose cheeks were stained with tears, but she didn't stop driving. Staring down at the two necklaces entangled together, I wondered if they were going to erase Given's memories. Would they take him away from me? All the memories that made him Given, the Martian boy who wore a half-cocked smile, who was always calm and sweet, and whose silver eyes lit up in a way that pumped solace into my veins. They couldn't just take him and erase him, not when I'd just made a place for him inside my heart. Madam scooped me into her arms, and my sobs shook us both.

"There's nothing you could have done, child," Madeline said as she stroked my shoulder.

"I c-c-could have ju—" I took a gulp of air. "—j-j-just..." I shook my head back and forth. "No. He can't be gone."

Madam righted me and wiped tears from my cheeks. She didn't say anything, just gazed at me in the most comforting way. I'd never seen her sapphire eyes look so soothing before.

But he's gone. Given's gone. That can't be.

"I'm so sorry, Janie," I whispered, trying to push my voice past the lump in my throat.

"I know Given," Janie said. Her voice had a slight quiver in it. "You wouldn't have been able to stop him."

I shook my head, knowing she was right but still feeling like I could have stopped him. I should have grabbed him and pulled him along with me, gripped his hand, clutched his arm, just not let him go. He was crazy, crazy for doing it for me.

Don't forget me. Please. His words whispered in my mind in an unbearable way, so soft and sweet like him. I just wanted to circle my arms around him, pull him close, and smell the cologne of aloe and soap on his shirt.

*

I awoke groggy and restless; my head was resting on Madam's lap. Night had fallen over the car, turning the cab pitch black. I sat up and looked around, trying to see past the darkness. The SUV was parked between two trees for camouflage. Everyone was fast asleep with small throw blankets draped across them. My body felt numb, and my throat felt raw with stale grief.

I saw a flicker of light from the corner of my eye and turned to see a set of headlights. My heart jumped, and I shook Madam's leg frantically.

"We have to go," I whispered.

"Huh? What?" Madam said, opening her eyes.

"We have to go."

Madam stiffened as the sight of the headlights instantly woke her.

"Janie," Madam said, shaking her shoulder.

She instantly jumped into an alert state.

"Do they see us?" she asked.

And as soon as the question had left her lips, my etching lit up, and a spotlight zeroed in on the SUV.

"They see us! Go!" Madam yelled.

Janie started up the engine and sped away. We raced down an open road. The vehicle with the bright headlights honked at us, as if that would make us stop. All of a sudden, a loud bang rang out from the rear, making the SUV jerk.

"What's going on, Janie?" Madam asked.

"I don't know," Janie said, glaring at the gauges on the SUV.

"Oh, no," I said when I saw something blinking on the bumper.

"Something's wrong," Janie said.

I glanced at the speedometer; we were slowing down.

"I think they did something to my car."

The SUV had stopped and wouldn't start up again. Janie kept turning the key, but the engine only sputtered a few times and then died. Madam threw open her door and pulled me out of the SUV with her. She ran off the open road, and we pushed our way through the forest. A car skidded to a stop and people ran after us.

"Hurry," Madam said, keeping a tight grip on my hand.

A Jeep sprang out from around a large fallen tree trunk, headlights beaming, spotlighting us. We turned around to go the other way, but figures holding large floodlights raced towards us. The Jeep skidded to a stop.

"No!" Madam yelled, throwing me behind her back, sandwiching me between herself and the trunk of a tree. "You can't have my child!"

"Don't worry," said a man. He moved slowly toward us, set down his floodlight, and lifted his palms up. He had russet skin, a shaved head, and a deep voice. His hands appeared to be empty.

"We'll explain everything, but first, we have to go," another man said. He had tanned skin, bleached white hair, and a flat voice.

"Get away from us!" Madam screamed.

"We need to go," the first man repeated.

"You need to leave us alone!" Madam shouted back.

"You have to trust us." Another male voice emerged from behind the wall of lights. "We are running out of time, Mom."

Madam's shoulders tensed further, as a tall, broad-shouldered man strutted towards us. As he stepped in front of the bright lights, he came into view. He had light brown hair, which was cut short and feathered as the breeze blew through it.

"Simon?"

He stepped closer and held up a light to his face. His eyes were bright green. Madam out to him but then pulled back and looked down at his pinstriped suit.

"You're a…a…" She couldn't get the words to leave her lips.

"Simon! Come on!" someone yelled.

"I know!" Simon shouted back.

"Tick tock! Tick tock!"

Simon looked down at his watch. "I'm sorry," he said, taking a step foward. "I'll explain later. I promise." He pulled a small flashlight out of his pocket and moved it toward Madam.

"No!" I said, remembering what the device was.

I started to cover Madam's eyes, but then Simon switched his target and flashed it at me. I didn't have enough time to protect myself. My eyes filled with white for a split second, melting my muscles, and I collapsed in Madam's arms.

"No!" Madam shouted. "What did you do?"

A woman stepped out of the Jeep, wearing jeans and a t-shirt.

"I'm sorry, Mom," Simon said, leaning over me.

"What did you do?" Madam gaped up at him.

"James, take my mom to the Jeep."

"What?" Madam shouted as the man with russet skin, James, pulled on her arm.

"Please explain to her what's going on," Simon said as he gripped me.

"No!"

James had to have his partner grab Madam's other arm. For a few seconds, I was in the middle of some strange tug-of-war, Madam against all of them, but they finally wrenched me from Madam's grasp. Everything felt hazy and distant.

"No! No!" Madam screamed as they pulled her into the Jeep.

Simon carried me through the forest, half-walking, half-running. The woman followed behind, glancing up at me every once in a while. Simon charged out of the forest and ran over to a van. Its sliding door was open and waiting for us. He hurried inside and placed me onto the floor, and they closed the door and started the engine. I tried to reach for the handle, but he just clutched my hand and rested it atop my stomach.

"We wasted a lot of precious time." The woman wearing the jeans had black hair and dark eyes and was holding a flashlight.

"I know," Simon said.

He pulled off his jacket and rolled up his sleeves. His arm was etched, but his etching had a deep, ridged line through the middle of it.

"Let..." I took a breath, trying to muster up enough strength. "Me go."

"Basil," he said, leaning closer to me, "I need you not to fight the sedative. Please."

"Awake or not, we're still doing it," the woman said. "We don't have a choice. Beam her again. Maybe you missed an eye."

Simon pulled the flashlight from his pocket. I swatted at him, but he just pushed my hands away. He pulled open my right eye, giving it a flash, and then my left. Everything suddenly felt far away and wrapped in a gauzy hue of white.

"I think it worked, Lindy," Simon said.

Her name hung in the air, calling out to me, reminding me of Bobby. She matched the exact description of her: long, dark brown hair, olive skin, and dark brown eyes. But that couldn't be her, because Lindy was dead.

"Good. We're here," she said, sliding open the door.

"Hurry up!" an angry man shouted. "I risked everything waiting for you!"

"Thank you," Simon said as he picked me up and ran.

I heard the whistling of a train, and struggled to crack my eyes open. There was an open train car, and people were waving for Simon to hurry up. He handed me up to two people, who pulled me onto the train.

"I don't understand why you're willing to risk so much for this girl. Why? Why is she so important?" the same angry man barked.

"That's none of your business," Simon said, his voice turning harsh. "Just get this train going, okay?"

"Bring her here," said a voice in the crowd as they pulled me away from the ledge.

They placed me onto a gurney. Floodlights hung from the walls of the car, swinging back and forth. Lindy dabbed at my inner elbow with something wet and cold.

"Nice," a man with curly black hair said as he pulled off my sweatband.

My etching was glowing again. Lindy inserted an IV into my arm; it burned when it broke past my skin.

"Almost prepped for surgery?"

"Surgery?" I barely pushed out. It sounded like the wind whispering.

My head rocked to the side. The weight of whatever the flashlight had done to me pulled it down.

"Shh, you're safe now." Simon whispered, pulling my face toward his. His green eyes lulled me even farther away.

Thirty-Nine

"Shh. You're safe now."

I was staring at a green set of eyes so vivid they shimmered like a gem in the sun. The creature dressed in white knelt in front of me as I sat on a cold metal chair.

"I'm going to get you out of here." The voice sounded male.

The creature looked around the room, empty save for a few chairs. He helped me up, but my muscles were too weak to manipulate, so the creature scooped me into his arms and headed out of the room. He slunk against the walls of a brightly lit hallway, clutching me close to his chest.

I heard a weird, quiet, metallic squeak. The sound grew louder, and the creature carrying me started looking around frantically for something. He was backpedaling, but he exhaled loudly when a little boy came into view. The boy had dark brown hair and was dragging an IV stand with him, as if he needed it to survive. The wheels to the stand squeaked as the little boy staggered in our direction.

"Hey," The creature whispered, kneeling down in front of the little boy.

"Hi," said the boy. The florescent lights bounced off his eyes, making them flicker bright silver.

The creature scanned the empty hallway and then pulled the IV from the boy's arm. He gripped his hand and started pulling him along with us. A keycard granted him access to several thick doors. He glanced down at me, giving me a flash of his vivid green eyes. We came to a door where he had to punch in a numeric code on a keypad. When he finished pressing the numbers, the keypad flashed red.

"What?" he whispered.

He tried again, but it did the same thing. He put me on the ground and unzipped his white jumpsuit, pulling out a small, white plastic box. Inside were small tools which he used to pull the keypad off the wall. As he played around with the wires, the door suddenly flew open, and the room filled with a blaring alarm.

"Come on," he said. "Time to go."

The creature threw me over his shoulder and gripped the boy's hand tighter. He began to run so fast that the boy was having trouble keeping up, but the creature kept pulling him along. I heard growling in the background and boots thudding. We were outside; the cold night pricked my skin. There was a woman waiting for him, holding up a piece of the fence. She stood tall with long, dark hair. Slipping through the metal fence, the creature carried me down rocky terrain. His foot slipped, and he stumbled in his steps until the woman righted him.

"Be careful," she whispered, her voice laced with warning and concern.

I suddenly realized we were climbing down the side of a mountain with only a two-foot-wide footpath to follow. We followed the woman down to an open Jeep, where the creature plopped me in the backseat, buckled me in, and then did the same with the boy. When we were all inside, the woman started the Jeep and raced down an open road.

No one talked as we sped down an unmarked road, visible only by the headlights. The wind flipped my hair and filled the Jeep with noise. It was as if everyone was too scared to make a sound. So no one said anything. An eternity passed before I heard a deep exhale escape from the creature's mouth.

"The code didn't work," he said, pulling off his white head covering, transforming him into an actual person with light brown hair.

"I told you not to do that, Simon."

"No," the creature—Simon—took a deep breath, as if he needed it to calm his nerves. "You said to do it only if I had to."

"We could've come back for her," she said.

"No, I couldn't have. They were about to transfer her," he said. "I wouldn't have been able to find her if they had moved her."

The woman took a breath and stole a quick peek at the boy. "Who's the extra cargo?"

"I don't know."

I looked over at the boy sitting next to me.

"You don't know?" She sounded angry.

"He was there, so I took him."

"This changes things," she said.

"This changes nothing."

"They're following us," the woman said, tapping her forearm.

Simon turned around and looked at my glowing arm and then at the boy's. He pulled off the necklace that was around his neck and he put it on the boy.

"Always keep these on," he said fiercely. "They will keep you safe."

The woman skidded to a stop at the edge of a forest. Simon jumped out of the jeep and lifted the boy out, setting him on the rocky ground.

"Thank you, Lindy," Simon said as he pulled me from the jeep.

"Run," she said and then sped away.

"Come on," said Simon, pulling the boy and me with him.

We ran through the woods, being tugged along by Simon's grip. The forest growled ominously. I could hear faint cracking and rustling of trees and underbrush. Then, suddenly, with the sound of breaking wood, Simon stopped moving.

"Aaaah! No!" Simon said, pulling on his leg.

The cracking and rustling was now joined by the sound of people charging through the forest. Simon pulled on his leg, but it was wedged inside jagged roots.

"You," Simon said, pointing to the boy. "Keep her safe. Run straight until you see a swamp. Hide in the large house." Simon tugged on his leg harder, grinding his teeth with each yank. "Wait for me." Simon looked back, hearing the crunching of leaves getting closer. "Go! Now!"

The boy and I looked at each other.

"They're coming for you! Run!" Simon screamed as he yanked at his boot frantically.

The boy gripped my hand and pulled me away from Simon, and I gave a small wave as we slipped between the trees.

Forty

I woke up feeling too cozy and too at ease. A beeping noise filled the background as my fingers felt the familiar softness of my bed. I opened my eyes slowly, and my crimson comforter came into view. I scanned the familiar walls and dark wooden door; I was in my bedroom. The room was empty, and monitors sat chirping on the side of my mattress. My head was woozy, like my brain detached itself from my spine.

As I sat up, my light brown hair fell off my shoulders, and I looked down at my hands. My etched arm was wrapped in gauze. I scooted to edge of the bed, threw my legs over and sat slumped over, staring down at gray sweatpants that weren't my own. My legs felt like noodles, and my head spun quicker. I put my hand to my forehead and saw wires attached to my arm.

"Grogginess is normal." I blinked up and saw Simon sitting off in the corner. "You might want to rest for today."

"You," I said, narrowing my eyes at him.

"You should lie back down," Simon said, standing up and taking a forward.

"Where is Madam?" I said, scooting back on my bed.

"Basil, take it easy," Simon said, drifting toward me.

"Erin, Bobby, Janie, Madeline—" I took a heavy gulp, stumbling off the opposite end of my bed, "Given? Where are they? What have you done to them?" I stumbled toward the door, feeling the IV and a wire yank off my arm. I gripped the arm as I knocked into a small table, one that Madam usually kept in the library. A plastic pitcher and ceramic mug clattered to the floor, spilling water across the hardwoods past Simon's sock-covered feet. The mug, one of Erin's favorites, broke in two.

"Everyone's fine." He took another step toward me with his hands up in a relenting fashion.

"What did you to me?" I shouted, pressing my hand to my head.

All of a sudden, the door opened.

"Need some help in here," Simon said to the person behind the door.

I backpedaled, crumpling to the ground when my shoulder hit the wall, and squeezed my eyes closed, bracing myself for... What? I didn't know.

"Basil." The voice was a familiar reedy one.

I looked up, and Madam's sapphire irises stared back at me.

"It's okay," she said, putting her hand on my upper arm.

"You're okay," I choked out.

I slumped into her chest, feeling so happy and so scared. I wrapped my arms around her, holding her with arms that felt like jelly.

"Basil," Erin's cooed next.

"Erin," I said, looking up. He stood there with a mug of fresh, steaming coffee.

"Where is everybody?" I asked, standing up on shaky limbs.

"Everyone's fine. Madeline is in her room. And Bobby, he's..." Erin glanced over at Simon for a quick second. "He's in the kitchen." His tone was slow, and his face was covered with concern.

"I want to see them," I said, staggering to the door and whipping it open.

I stumbled out of the room and crashed into something soft and warm.

"Whoa there. You're always beating me up." The voice was soothing and enticing.

I gripped the warm, sturdy wall and looked up. Given's eyes were shining bright silver, a wonderfully extraterrestrial color. He helped right me and then pulled me into his arms.

"Hey there, fair maiden," he whispered into my hair.

"Hey," I whispered back. "Are you okay?"

"Dizzy, but overall quite copacetic." He gazed down at me with that half-cocked smile. Only he could throw out a word like that at a time like this.

I smiled. "Is your Mom okay?"

"I'm fine," Janie said as she approached.

From the corner of my eye, I saw Simon step out of the room. I quickly turned around, which only made my head spin more.

"Everything's okay."

"I need answers," I said flatly, trying to stand straight.

"And I said I would give them to you."

"Who are you people? What do you want? Why did you erase our memories? Where are we from?"

"Whoa, hold up. I'm not who you think I am. I'm not one of those extraction agents."

"You're not with the men in the pinstriped suits?"

Given supported his body against the wall, eyeing Simon cautiously.

"No," Simon said, shaking his head.

I looked over at Erin and Madam, and they confirmed with a nod.

"What did you do to us?" Given asked, holding up his bandaged forearm, shaking his head as if to clear it.

"We deactivated your cuffs, so they can't track you. We did it to help you hide."

"Hide? Why?" Given asked.

"Why do they want us?" I asked.

"Wait," Simon said, holding up his hand. "Let's just start from the beginning. Hi, I'm Simon." He held his hand out to me.

"Hi," I whispered, staring at his hand like I was waiting for it to bite me.

After a few awkward seconds, he dropped his hand. I glanced over at Erin and Madam, and their faces looked happy. More than happy. Elated. Madam gripped my shoulder with a soft but sturdy hand. I looked back at Simon, examining his features closely. He was their son; there was no question in my mind about that. His small smile resembled Madam's, and his light, brown hair looked like Erin's had before it lost its pigmentation.

Simon's smile grew broad and bright, making his green eyes flicker. He took a deep breath and said, "I'm your brother."

ABOUT THE AUTHOR

I write to give my literary lungs a stretch – to express and explore. I write because I'm a dork that's addicted to rich words, suspenseful stories, and massive amounts of coffee. So, people can be whisked away for as long as their nose is safely tucked inside my story. For the teenager that's trapped inside my body that clamors for more pages to read. I write out of pure insanity, weirdoness, and overall, love.

7201400R00148

Made in the USA
San Bernardino, CA
26 December 2013